Duke

ι

The Ghosts of Poynter

Chase Tyler is headed for the town of Poynter. An attempted ambush, the death of an innocent man, and a sheriff who won't play by the rules, added to a brother-in-law who can't be trusted, and a young man out for vengeance, all make for a pretty complicated visit. When Chase also meets a woman who bears more than a passing resemblance to Chase's lost love there is very little hope of him laying old ghosts to rest.

The Ghosts of Poynter

Amos Carr

A Black Horse Western

ROBERT HALE · LONDON

© Amos Carr 2012
First published in Great Britain 2012

ISBN 978-0-7090-9542-2

Robert Hale Limited
Clerkenwell House
Clerkenwell Green
London EC1R 0HT

www.halebooks.com

Typeset by
Derek Doyle & Associates, Shaw Heath
Printed and bound in Great Britain by
CPI Antony Rowe, Chippenham and Eastbourne

CHAPTER ONE

Almost silently, giving thanks for the night sounds which would cover any small noises he might make, Chase Tyler crept forward through the trees, towards the small orange glow of the campfire.

The small stand of trees was perched close to the edge of a shallow ravine, through which a wide, slow river flowed. An ideal place: wood for the fire, fresh water to hand, plenty of wild life to be had for the catching, and an untidy, natural clearing, close to the cliff edge, just big enough for a small camp.

Chase had smelled the smoke from some way off; Wilson was getting careless. Seemed like he reckoned he was far enough away from any posse now, so he could let his guard down. He was making no attempt to hide from anyone, or to disguise his whereabouts in any way. He was getting lazy. Never a good thing when you were on the run.

Chase could smell the smoke from the fire, mixing with tobacco smoke, strong coffee, and spit-roast coney. Wilson was settling in for the night, believing he was safe.

Chase stayed low in the brush; it was a darkening night, made even darker under the trees, good for hiding, waiting;

he was patient, he could wait for as long as it took. Until morning if needed.

He knew his prey was totally unaware that he was being watched; he was hunkering down for the night. His horse and mule were hobbled near by, his rifle lay close, and he'd kept his gunbelt on. The saddle-bags, which he was using as his pillows, were obviously full of the bank's money. He gave a self-satisfied little groan as he laid his head on them, pulled the blanket over himself, and tugged his hat down over his eyes.

The fire was dying, and so was the light, but Chase needed little more than the weak moonbeams flitting between the branches. His eyes were well trained to low light by now. He'd hunted men before, quite often by night. Usually for money. No, only for the money. It was a way to get by.

Bounty hunting wasn't his favourite job, but it paid well, and this job would be very well paid. He'd had an advance; the rest would be his when he brought Wilson in, dead or alive. Alive was preferable, it paid better. Dead paid, although not quite as well. One way or the other Joe Wilson would soon be arriving at Coyote Springs sheriff's office.

Wilson and three of his cronies had killed five people in a hold-up at the town bank. They'd started a fire before they left, so the townsfolk would be busy; even so, the other three had been killed as they tried to escape from the town. With most of the town sidetracked into trying to put out the blaze, Wilson had got clean away.

Chase had ridden into Coyote Springs the day after the robbery. Tongues were still wagging. He'd offered his services, and been accepted. The sheriff and his posse had been out trying to find Wilson, without any luck. Sheriff Jackson could see that Tyler was a man well used to this kind of work, and he was desperate to find the town's money, so he'd rapidly accepted the help offered. There was a poster on his office wall for Wilson, who'd held up another four banks over the last couple of years.

Chase spent a day around town, checking stories, asking questions. He stocked up on provisions, formulated his plan, informed the sheriff where he was headed, and lit out. That was almost a week back, and now, he'd finally got Wilson in his sights.

This was the moment Chase didn't relish, deciding whether to move in now, or hang around until daylight to take his prey on. He cautiously moved forward, low to the ground. That decision was taken out of his hands suddenly, when, high in the tree to his left, a hoot owl, disturbed by his small movement, let out a loud shrieking alarm call, and flew off with a noisy flapping of wings.

Instantly, Wilson was up on his feet, pulling his gun. Chase was faster, he'd had his Colt drawn, and the hammer cocked even before the owl's hoot, having decided to go in immediately, and not wait until Wilson was fresh in the morning.

'Drop it, Wilson!'

Wilson ignored the warning and let off a shot. Chase had seen what was coming and neatly avoided it, shooting Wilson in the shoulder of his gun arm. The outlaw dropped his gun to the ground and clutched at his arm, but almost at once he lunged towards his rifle, left arm outstretched to grab it. Chase fired off another two rounds in quick succession. One of them hit the dirt in front of Wilson, covering him with dust and pine needles, the other grazed his outstretched hand.

Wilson screamed in fury as he drew back his hand. Placing bleeding hand to bleeding shoulder, he charged at

Chase like an angry bull, looking to knock him to the ground and overpower him. Chase saw what was coming, and sidestepped. Wilson hit a tree with his head.

Staggering backwards, and swearing loudly, the outlaw slumped to the ground, shaking his head. Chase stood over him, gun in hand, ready for the next move.

'You done, Wilson?'

'You bastard!'

'That's not nice, I was going to let you ride into Coyote Springs. Now I guess I might just let you walk back there. Hands behind your back.' He motioned with his gun.

Wilson realized he wasn't going anywhere now, and painfully managed to get his hands behind him, where Chase bound them tightly, ignoring the outlaw's cries of pain. He tied the man's legs together, heaved him over to the campfire, and threw him down beside the saddle-bags he'd been resting on a moment ago.

Chase went and unhobbled the man's animals, he loaded up the mule, and saddled the roan. He untied Wilson's legs, stood him up, and tied a rope to his hands, ignoring the blood creeping down the man's arm. It was a clean shot; he'd live, unfortunately. Chase climbed up on the roan and kicked it into a walk.

'Keep up, Wilson, or you'll be dragged through this here brush.'

The outlaw let out a stream of profanities, but began walking beside the horse, tripping over branches and careering into the horse's side as they went. He continued to rant about what he'd do to his captor as soon as he got his hands on him. Chase ignored the man's noise for a while, then he drew the horse to a halt, pulled out his gun, and drew a bead on the outlaw.

'OK Wilson. The sheriff said dead or alive. I reckon

dead'll do. Less'n you shut up. Hell, you're gonna hang anyways; might as well save them the job, eh?'

Wilson shook his head quickly, and shut his mouth almost as quickly. They carried on their journey in comparative silence to the end of the tree line, where Chase had left his own mount so that he would make no sounds whilst moving in on the outlaw's camp. There, he dismounted from the roan, helped Wilson to get on board it, tied a rope from the outlaw's mount to his own saddle horn, and swung up on to his stallion.

'OK boy, let's get this sack of entrails over to Coyote Springs.'

He wasn't looking forward to having to spend a few days in the outlaw's company, and, worse still, a few nights having to watch his back in case the varmint tried to make a run for it, though he doubted Wilson would try much, with a bust-up shoulder and shot-up hand.

Still, Chase was none too comfortable. He pushed on faster than he would normally have done in order to get back to the town in double quick time. They made camp twice, and each time Chase trussed Wilson up like a saddle blanket for the night, gagging him to stop his endless profanities, and get at least some shut eye.

They arrived back in Coyote Springs, where they were met by the sheriff and a group of townsfolk all wanting to shake Chase's hand, and to string up Wilson there and then. The sheriff and his deputy relieved Chase of his prisoner, and they all headed for the jailhouse. As soon as Wilson was in a cage he started throwing his profanities around again, aimed at the sheriff, at Chase, the good townsfolk, anyone and everyone.

Chase pulled his gun in the blink of an eye, and quickly rushed to the cell, aiming right between Wilson's eyes.

'Steady on, Mr Tyler,' the sheriff said sternly. 'You can't shoot a man in custody.'

'The hell I can. He's driven me plumb crazy with his profanities all the way in here. I reckon I've just about had enough.'

He pulled back the hammer. Wilson cowered in the corner, calling out to the sheriff to stop the man. The sheriff sighed loudly,

'On the other hand, I guess it'll save us all the fuss of a hangin'. Oh, go ahead, Tyler. I'll look the other way. Say the gun went off by accident.'

The sheriff walked over to his desk in the front office, leaving Wilson to Chase and his Colt. Wilson had wet himself and a dark patch was spreading across the front of his already dirty pants. Chase laughed. He released the hammer and holstered his gun.

'Hell, I ain't about to shoot a kid who wets his diapers.'

He turned on his heels and went out to join the sheriff, who was counting coins into a poke. He smiled as he handed it over.

'Well deserved, young man. Y'know, I really would have looked the other way back there. Wilson deserves it. I'm surprised you didn't just finish him off on the trail; you'd've been paid even if he'd been dead.'

'Yeah, I know that, but I don't hold with killin' a man in cold blood, less'n there's no other way. Besides, your townsfolk have lost kin to him and his gang. They deserve to see justice done right here, so they can ease their grief. I'd best be off.'

'Tyler, you're a good man. On behalf of the folks of Coyote Springs who lost kin to that snake, I thank you.'

Chase touched his hat in salute and left the office, went over to the telegraph office and sent a wire, then mounted

10

his horse and headed out of town. He was heading towards Poynter, to visit with his family.

CHAPTER TWO

The black stallion skeetered off sideways. Tossing his head, eyes rolling, snorting loudly, he half-reared, dropping low on his hocks, fore hoofs pawing the air, the sudden action almost unseating his half-dozing rider.

Chase Tyler, around a rein's width short of six feet in height, and almost as broad-shouldered, let out a loud curse as one of his feet left the stirrup, and he instinctively balanced himself up by tightening the grip of his long legs on the prancing animal's sides.

It was his own fault; he should have been concentrating on the path, not daydreaming. A man could get himself killed that way. He was trail-weary though; the ride here had been a long one. His temper flared up uncharacteristically.

'Dammit boy! What in the hell's the matter with you?'

Had he been paying more attention to the path that lay ahead of them he'd have seen the big old rattler probably even before the horse did, and they could have cut an alternative track through the dry arroyo. The horse knew, instinctively, that the diamondback was the deadliest snake around; a mere graze from its virulent fangs could kill a horse, or a steer, never mind a man.

Chase, who sported a head of thick, unruly black curls, a

crooked smile, and the brightest blue eyes many a girl had ever seen, had spent the best part of his life to date picking up any kind of work he could, whenever and wherever it came, often way out in the wilderness areas. He was used to living on just his wits, and sparse rations. This way of life suited him well. He was searching, always searching. He'd been searching for so long now that he often forgot what it was he'd been looking for.

The strong planes of his face, tanned by long exposure to all weathers, were all but hidden now by a two-week-old growth of beard. Beneath the rim of his battered and stained old Stetson, his eyes shone wide and bright, and, despite a rather tired look right now, they never missed anything. To miss just one small item could mean the difference between living and dying.

With a wisdom way beyond his almost thirty years of life he surveyed his world. There was a somewhat haunted look behind his eyes; a restless, searching soul looked out. His muscular build, quiet, dark strength and calm manner were usually more than enough to deflect a difficult confronta-tion, often long before it had the chance to explode into something more sinister.

Chase sat light and easy in the saddle. Centaur-like, looking as though he were part of the horse, at home on any kind of saddle, or on none at all, it showed in his bearing, and the way he relaxed his own body almost into that of the animal. He could feel the horse's every move, and the small-est twitch of the powerful muscles beneath his body, almost as easily as he felt his own.

With Black in particular he felt a real and positive accord, one which he had never felt with any other horse. They had been through a hell of a lot together, and the deep trust which they now had, each in the other, was second to none.

13

As a youngster, he'd seen the magnificent horses used by the Cavalry, their muscular quarters, solid, thick necks, and bright intelligent eyes, made them stand out among other horses. He knew, even back then, that he'd be getting himself a Morgan one day.

Well-defined muscles, alert ears, and long, full manes and tails, made the Morgan a good-looking horse, as well as one that would be able to take on any type of terrain, and most jobs asked of it, without fear or hesitation. They weren't the largest horses around, standing just short of sixteen hands, but what they lacked in stature they made up for, many times over, in pure muscle, guts, and sheer brain-power. They were a breed to be reckoned with.

When he eventually found the animal some instinct had kicked in; he knew this was it. He'd been working at a black-smith's, in some hick, no-name town, when he'd paused in his hammering long enough to hear the smith haggling with someone.

Chase looked up from his work. The horse was tired-looking, razor-thin, head hanging low, eyes dull and almost lifeless, black coat dirty, harsh and staring. All sure signs of serious and prolonged maltreatment. His ribs and pin bones stuck out so that he looked like a walking skeleton; he was limping on his left foreleg and there were scars scattered all across his body.

The sorry-looking animal was being led, or rather dragged, by a thick rope harness, which was cutting into his face, pulled along by a dirty and disreputable looking character, who stank of beer and stale urine. Chase watched the horse; it was a stallion, but there was no fight left in it, no fire in its belly. It was starving to death, and too weak to do anything other than follow lamely where it was pulled, until it would finally have dropped.

It looked completely unpromising. Chase could sense that there was something special about it, even in such a sorry state. That it was a Morgan was in no doubt, Chase could see that, despite the maltreatment it had suffered, and when the smith shook his head, and sent the man on his way with a sneer, Chase left the smithy, stopped him, and asked him a few questions.

He was pretty sure that the drifter, who said he'd won the animal in a game of cards, did actually own the horse. There were no brands anywhere on it, Army or otherwise. In any case, Chase knew he was going to have the animal, even if only to save it from starving to death at the hands of the itinerant.

He stroked its soft, velvety muzzle, and as their eyes met, and the dying beast held his gaze with a still proud glint to its sad eyes, Chase immediately felt something pass between them. It was a feeling similar to that which he'd only felt one time before. It was that same feeling which kept him restless, trying to rediscover that once known 'something', which always seemed to be just beyond his reach.

He'd paid the asking price for the animal straight off, without any haggling. The old drifter couldn't believe his good fortune. Spitting on the coins for luck, he thrust them into his ragged shirt pocket, immediately crossed the street, and walked straight into the first saloon he came to. Chase watched him go, holding on to the rope tied round the horse's thin head.

The blacksmith laughed when he saw that Chase had purchased the wreck of an animal.

'You'll never do anything with that sorry-looking cayuse, Tyler. It'll be dead in a week. If'n you'd wanted a decent horse, you should have asked. I could have fixed you up with a good 'un. That feller's just gonna cause trouble. He's probably not even broke, and if'n you do manage to feed him up, he'll never let you ride him, not after what he's been through. Don't waste your time on him, he's only fit for crow-bait. Sell him on again, real quick. Better still, shoot him and feed the buzzards.'

'Oh, I reckon he'll surprise both of us, Phil. There's something about him. I'll get him cleaned up, and fed well, and he'll do me just fine.'

The smith snorted, shrugged, and went back to his work without another look at the animal. Chase led it to the corral behind the smithy, fed and watered it, watching carefully as it took deep, desperately thirsty draughts from the trough. The horse was jet black beneath the grime and dust, and when Chase checked its teeth he could see that the stallion was almost three years old. In his prime and ready for gentling.

After he'd had the horse for a while, and its general condition had improved enough for him to start working on it, Chase could tell it was only half-broken. His first thought had been to call it 'Diablo', the Devil, but then the horse turned out to be so biddable that the name didn't suit, so Chase simply ended up calling it 'Black'.

Whilst Black would do anything his new owner asked of him, no-one else could touch him. The stallion just didn't trust any other man. Chase invested a lot of time and effort over the next couple of years, getting the horse into tip-top condition, training it just the way he wanted it. Now they were inseparable, and he trusted the animal with his life, especially in such rough terrain as they were passing through at present.

He knew the Morgan was well able to pick his own way easily through the rocky gulches; Black was just about as sure-footed as a mountain goat. Horses have a knack not given to men, of finding paths where none exists; that is especially true of the Morgan.

Chase had trained Black to a hackamore: a bitless bridle; he didn't believe in hard-mouthing his animals, reckoning that without a bit a horse was even more responsive to its rider. He knew he'd never had such a good horse as this, and knew that he would never again see his like. The stallion would work until he dropped if Chase asked him to.

There was a strong, even almost psychic, bond between animal and man; each one seemed to know what the other was thinking; it was as if they were made from the same material. Now the man felt safe enough with the stallion to allow himself the occasional, and rare, pleasure of day-dreaming, letting his thoughts drift where they would, as his mount carried him steadily onward.

Chase could sense the steady, rolling, movement of the muscles beneath the heavy saddle as they rode along in almost total silence, only broken by the rhythmic sound of hoofs wending their way along the trail. There were small sparking taps as Black's metal shoes struck gently against rough scree. Almost the only other sounds to be heard were the soft creak and brush of the leather, and the breathing of man and animal in complete unison.

The air was fresh, clear, and, as yet anyway, these parts were completely untainted by the hand of any man. Breathing this pure air was just like drinking a good wine, and it could make you almost as heady if you weren't used to it.

Chase savoured these moments; the peace and quiet was like some kind of powerful medicine, keeping him sane in an often all too insane world. This time though, the day-dreams he had been indulging in had been rudely interrupted.

Calming the prancing horse, and his own heart, Chase watched the big old diamondback. It was just as scared of them as Black had been of it, as it slid swiftly and sinuously away into the dark crevice of a large rock. It had been catching the heat of the day, sunbathing on the rough scree, its intricate markings blending with its surroundings perfectly. Now it was getting restless, as the cool of the evening was drawing in. A horse approaching a little too close had sent the snake searching for cover for the night, setting up its loud warning rattle as it did so.

As quickly as it had come, the man's anger subsided. He knew it wasn't Black's fault, it was his alone. They were both tired; they should have made camp on the trail last night. However, his provisions were all but done, so working against his usually much better judgement, he'd made Black push on. He slapped the horse fondly on its neck, trail dust rising up in a swirling grey cloud from the hard, muscled hide.

'Easy there, old feller, he's gone now, take it easy.'

His steady voice calmed the animal, it eased its prancing, skirted the place where the rattler had disappeared, and pushed on, as eager as its master to pass through this rough and rocky place, and reach the open plains.

Neither of them liked enclosed spaces; there were too many dangers, and not enough space to move fast if trouble threatened. As Black's steady gait carried them onwards Chase eased himself up in the saddle, standing high in the stirrups, stretching, and straightening his long legs.

His back was stiff, his throat was dry, and his belly was grumblingly empty.

Thank the Lord that Poynter was just a couple of miles up ahead now. He could get himself a decent bath and shave, bank his money, stock up on provisions, and catch up on all the latest news. It'd been some time since he'd last visited Poynter. His sister, Annelise, two years older than he, still lived there with her husband, Bill, and their children. Chase and his sister had spent a good part of their lives there growing up.

He had been courting a local girl back then, Jess McCloud, a sassy little thing. Long, curling hair, red as a desert sunset, with a scattering of freckles across her tip-tilted nose. Her eyes were as green as the fresh spring grass, and she had a smile just as bright as a new dawn.

There was no shortage of admirers real keen to make her acquaintance. However, it was Chase she'd really taken a fancy to. And he, in his turn, was well and truly smitten. Her pa ran the Lazy M, but didn't make much cash from the spread; he was a heavy drinker and quickly boozed away any money he did make, all the time sinking ever deeper into debt.

He treated his wife and two daughters real bad, and didn't approve of Chase seeing his elder girl. The girl's sister was two years younger than Jess; they'd seen a lot in their young lives, mostly things kids that age shouldn't have to see. There was a little boy too, just a babe in arms at the time.

Jess had to take her little sister almost everywhere with her, even sometimes when she'd arranged to meet Chase. It was safer for both girls if they were out of the house when their father was in one of his drunken rages. Then their mother would put the baby in his cradle in a corner of the room, to keep him safe. She couldn't avoid her husband's vicious beatings, but she could try and make sure the children were out of harm's way.

When Jess's father found out about Chase he'd beaten his daughter black and blue, more than once, but at seventeen she was an independent, fiery little creature, and had quickly made up her mind that Chase was the man for her. She was damn well going to carry on seeing him, beatings regardless. Chase knew he was no physical match for McCloud in a fistfight, not yet, so even though his thoughts kept turning to the best way to rid them of the old man, he knew he couldn't do it.

Chase and Jess both knew he would come off worse in any confrontation with the bigger, harder man. Especially if McCloud was drunk. And he was nearly always drunk. So Chase had to keep quiet, hold his anger in, and hold on to Jess's bruised and battered body, soothing her wounds as best he could, stroking her ruby curls as she cried out her pain.

Chase was determined that one day he was going to find a way of releasing Jess from her prison. One day there would be a way. One day he would be strong enough.

They'd resorted to meeting in secret. Chase was as besotted as any teenage boy could ever get. His heart did back flips when he knew he was going to be meeting Jess, and he was often almost completely tongue-tied in her company.

He reckoned that if that was what love was like, he must be in it. Real deep.

They'd shared some real warm and tender moments together in the old barn, or down in the little valley, close to the stream, on the rare occasions when Jess could escape without her sister. For a boy who'd never experienced sex before, he had to reckon that it was just about the best thing in the whole darned world.

'I'll always love you, Chase. No matter what.' Jess murmured into his shoulder, as they lay curled deep in the hay one warm afternoon. She was gently playing with the black curls on his chest as he scattered small kisses all over her shoulder and neck.

'You know I'm going to love you for ever, Jess. For ever. I could never feel this way about anybody else, ever.' Chase replied, stroking her firm breasts softly as he pulled her once more into his eager, embrace.

He'd even harboured serious thoughts of marriage back then, but he couldn't seem to get up the raw courage he needed to ask for her hand.

Fear of her angry and abusive father was probably one of the main reasons. No. If he was to be truthful, it was *the* main reason. But there was time yet, and he would ask her, oh yes he would, one day. Then they'd get as far away from her father as they possibly could.

Gradually McCloud had sold off small parcels of their land to those spreads adjoining the M, but instead of paying off his debts with the money he raised, he simply went straight to the saloon, and drank it all away.

One summer night, after a particularly heavy drinking session, he staggered out of the bar, just about managed to get himself mounted crookedly on his sorry-looking horse, and rode homeward, none too steady in the saddle, singing tunelessly and loudly as he went.

Chase was at the bar that night, and had watched him go, anger surging through him, knowing the women were going to be in for another hell-filled night, and wishing with all his heart that the old man would fall off his horse and break his neck. Or worse. Maybe Chase would just go and help him on his way, the thought ran through his tormented mind. McCloud's old horse knew the way home, which was good, because, left to his owner, they'd have probably ended up some place in Mexico.

In the early hours of the morning, the townsfolk were woken by loud shouting. The whole sky seemed to be aglow, and was dancing with orange and red flames. Thick smoke was drifting in heavy, billowing, dark-grey clouds towards the town. The Lazy M was on fire!

Practically the whole town turned out to try and save the family and the house. McCloud wasn't anyone's favourite person, not by any means, and there were many who cruelly reckoned that there was really no point in saving him. But his wife and youngsters were in there too, and they sure did need help.

However, by the time the townsfolk had arrived out at the spread it was all too obvious to everyone there. There was nothing at all that they could have done. The house was almost gone, the crackling flames were eating more of it by the second. It had been a much hotter summer than usual; everything was tinder dry, and it wasn't long before the raging fire had taken a hold of the whole place.

By the time the first men had reached the ranch the barn to the side of the house had collapsed in on itself, became a black skeleton of charred and smoking remains, and the fire was crackling, dancing, and roaring, like a living thing, among the heavy, dry framework.

Orange, red and yellow flames were leaping and moving like some ravenous beast; white, yellow, and red sparks were shooting high up into the night sky, the fire was eating its way through the timbers as though they were just match-sticks.

It was a sight that many there thought must be what Hell itself looked like.

Any stock that might have been in the barn had either died in the inferno, or managed to escape and run off. They were the last thing on anyone's mind. There were four people in there to be saved. Men found feed buckets, ladles, even used their hats, hurriedly drawing water from the old trough in the yard. They ran back and forth, a chain of darkly animated grotesque silhouettes against the glow of the blaze, in a vain and desperate effort to try to quench the greedy, out of control, flames.

Nobody could even attempt to go into the blazing building to try and save the occupants. No one could possibly have got out of there alive. Some of the men were anxiously searching the surrounding area, calling out frantically to the family, just in case anyone had managed to get out. Chase was desperate. He searched everywhere, in all their 'special' places, anywhere that his beloved Jess might have run, or worse, crawled, off to.

He ran around calling out her name for long after it was obvious that there was no one left alive anywhere. There were no trees nearby to worry about them catching fire, it was just low scrub and bare earth, with a few scattered boulders. Just maybe though, someone could have taken shelter behind one of them.

The desperate calls of Chase and the other townsfolk were answered only by the louder crackling of the flames. They had tried real hard to put out the fire, but when the sheriff had turned up, and sadly shaken his head, declaring: 'It's too far gone folks, there's nobody left in there now, that's for sure,' they had to admit there was nothing else to be done, and sadly, gradually, they drifted off to their own homes, away from the smouldering heap of ash, and charred skeletons of the beams.

They went reluctantly, ones and twos at a time, muttering together, knowing it was true, but first damping down everything around the house, making sure that the flames weren't going to spring back into life, or worse, spread any further and endanger the small town.

Chase's father and a couple of friends had taken the boy home between them. Or rather, they half-walked, half-carried him. Distraught, and overcome with grief, he kept struggling against them, half-falling to his knees, screaming out in despair, trying desperately to get back to look for Jess. The men knew that he needed to be as far away as possible from the remains of the Lazy M right now, and back with his own family.

The sheriff left two of his deputies behind to keep watch for a while, and to see if they could save any possessions that might miraculously have been spared. There was nothing left though, bar a heap of cooling grey ash. The eventual verdict was that it had simply been a tragic accident. The old man must have tried to light a cigarette; he was so far in the bottle that he'd dropped the match. The whole family had been overcome in their beds by the thick, black, choking smoke, and the place had gone up so quick then, that even if they had woken, there would have been very little chance anyone would have been able to get out.

Chase had been totally and completely devastated by the loss of Jess: the first real, deep, tortured, loss of his young life.

He'd grieved for months then, knowing, in some place down inside of him, that he'd never feel like that about anyone else again. Knowing, with a deep and powerful certainty that, no matter what might come along in his life, he was never going to take himself any other woman.

He'd never stop loving Jess. No matter what life might throw at him.

He took to going off out of town on his own, kicking at the rocks, throwing stones at anything and nothing, shooting at dried branches, birds, trees. Dropping to his knees, and beating at the ground with his fists until they bled. Screaming his grief out into the emptiness. Looking for answers. Looking for Jess. Everywhere and anywhere, whilst, at the same time knowing he would never see her beautiful pale face, and tumbling red curls ever again.

The desperate, sharp, pain of a deep and terrible loneliness filled him completely; it filled the air around him, and ate him up with its misery. It filled up his soul with darkness, and made its home in his heart.

He decided not to stick around Poynter after that, but to go off and look for his own way in the world. He took his buckskin horse, the old Colt his father had given him on his fourteenth birthday, and a few possessions, and lit out, despite his father's dire warnings, and his mother's tearful protests, and without any real idea of where he would go; or indeed, even of what he was going to do to make ends meet. He was almost nineteen now, almost a man. It was time now for him to become his own man.

Sometimes, some of the things he'd done along his lonely way had meant he was on the wrong side of the law. Chase Tyler was a free agent, taking what work he could, wherever he could find it, stockman, wrangler, fencer, trapper, logger, even sometime bounty hunter, just about anything that would pay for his next meal. He'd done things, once in a while, that he'd never want to do again, and things he knew he'd probably have to do again, like it or not.

Somehow or other, even though a fair few of those jobs had come up somewhat short of legal, it didn't really matter. Legal or illegal, he was careful, and had never yet actually been *caught* doing anything that was outside of the law. Sure, he'd killed a few men. But only when really necessary; he mostly tried not to get himself into situations where a shoot-out was the only way out.

Every once in a while, whenever he was near enough on his travels, he'd head back to Poynter to visit with his family. He'd visit the town's bank whilst he was there too, to deposit whatever spare cash he might have in his poke at the time. This was one of those times.

His sister, Annelise, had married Bill Murdoch, who'd been born in the next town, Jonesville, but moved out as soon as he was of age. He came back down from up in the North when he moved to Poynter, on the search for the gold that was rumoured to have been found there.

He didn't find the gold; there was none but fool's gold there, but he found, and married, Annelise, and although he was twelve years older than she, they had her parents' blessing. Not long after the wedding the couple opened the new general store.

Their first child was born a little over a year later, and Chase's parents were completely delighted with their new grandchild. Less than a year after that, Chase's parents were killed in a freak accident, when the buckboard they were driving to Jonesville hit a boulder and overturned. He hadn't known about their deaths until he turned up for one of his infrequent visits home, only to find that they had been laid to rest in the small graveyard outside town, some six months before.

He was deeply saddened, and angry then. He visited their graves to pay his respects. Then he withdrew from the world once more, like he had after the fire, riding off, and disappearing again into the wilderness. He travelled the country from end to end, and back again, in a restless quest for some sort of peace. For an end to his everlasting grieving.

However, the ties to his sister were strong. She was the only living person he still had any real connection to; he was drawn back to the small town again and again, and would continue to be so until either he or his sister were dead.

'Hell, it must be nigh on a twelvemonth now since we saw 'em last, eh feller?'

The stallion snorted, as if in answer, his expressive ears moving back and forth, listening to his master's voice. Chase settled himself back lightly into the saddle, and stroked the thick, long, mane absently. The last time he'd been here Annelise had been expecting again, her fourth. It'd be a babe in arms now. He thought the world of his sister and her children; he couldn't say the same for her husband Bill, though.

He and Chase had been at daggers drawn since the moment they'd set eyes on each other. Chase had a sneaking, gut feeling that there was something not quite right about Bill Murdoch, but try as he might, he just couldn't lay his finger on it. As far as Chase could tell, Annelise and the kids wanted for nothing, and they seemed to be OK with Bill, so Chase was polite, but endeavoured to keep out of his brother-in-law's way as much as possible.

Bill knew, only too well, that Chase disapproved of him; the feeling was well and truly mutual. The pair of them almost visibly bristled like fighting cocks when in one another's presence. Bill could only hope that his brother-in-law would be riding out again pretty soon, as he usually did, and not hanging around any longer than might be necessary. Bill really didn't want him poking around where he wasn't wanted. He tried to keep as far away from Chase as possible whenever he came around.

Sometimes, however, Annelise, in a heroic but vain effort to create some kind of bond, or even just an unarmed and uneasy truce between them, ordered everyone to sit down for a meal together. To please her, because they both loved her, and only for that reason, they did as they were told, like penitent children.

Those meals were awkward affairs, heavily filled with stilted conversation, and artificially good manners, and all

27

the time the two men sat and glared at one another like sulking children, while Annelise sat with folded arms and glared at each of them in turn.

The two eldest kids, Charlie, eight, and Mary, six, always pestered Chase for tales of his exploits, and he usually obliged, albeit with very watered-down stories, even though Charlie was starting to demand much more information than Annelise really thought was good for him.

Chase gave Bill the benefit of the doubt on these occasions; maybe the older man simply wanted a few more adventures himself before he retired to his rocking-chair. Chase really couldn't help it, but it seemed like he just kept on rubbing Bill's nose in it by telling the kids all about his travels.

He didn't feel able to settle down anywhere, and just kept telling himself he had itchy feet disease. There had been a few times now though, when he was riding a long and lonely trail, that his mind wandered towards his sister and her brood, and what he himself might have had, once. In those rare times a rolling wave of loneliness overtook him.

He pretty soon shook himself out of those moods though; didn't do to go getting too maudlin when you were riding alone in the wilderness for so long. The nightmares would catch up to you then, and turn you crazy. He'd met men who'd been turned crazy by the wilderness nightmares. Destined to live and die a lonely, sad existence. Not for Chase though, he wasn't about to let that loneliness get to him.

Annelise and Bill certainly seemed settled enough, and he had to admit that he envied them that. The children weren't scared of Bill; Chase had seen the way they ran to greet their father when he came home, there was no fear, only love, in their eyes.

However, he still couldn't it get out of his head, a feeling that there was something about Bill which somehow wasn't quite 'right'.

Funnily enough, he'd been thinking of his brother-in-law back then, when the rattler had spooked Black. He'd been trying his best to put a finger on what it might be that had caused such animosity between the two of them. It had always eluded him, but he knew he was going to find out one day; he was a very patient man.

CHAPTER THREE

His mind had been shaken back into something like full wakefulness now. They'd be in Poynter soon, and then he'd have to be someone he wasn't: he'd do that for Annelise and the kids, but one day he'd find out just what it was about his brother-in-law that needled him so badly.

The jagged silhouette of the small town drew closer, and Chase could feel the horse's pace increase a little beneath him. Black needed a good rest too, and remembered this place of old; he instinctively knew that a warm stable and good food were close.

Chase settled back down into the saddle and rode easy, with loose reins, and with the quiet and confident strength of a man who knew just who he was, and was pretty comfortable with that knowing. With an almost inaudible click of his tongue, the man urged his mount onward. The horse lengthened his stride and began a steady, comfortably rocking gallop.

The night began to close in around them, blue fading to navy, and heading for black. A few clouds were about, some stars dotting the huge navy spread, but there was not much of a moon yet. It was a comforting sight to see the lights of the little town ahead going on one by one, beckoning the weary traveller onward.

The scent of the night air had changed a little now, even so far out of the town, Chase could still smell it. It was civilization.

Like wine, there was a certain nose about civilization. It was totally different from the open range, and certainly completely different from the wilderness areas he loved so much.

There was smoke and sweat in civilization, there were cattle and horses, beer and heat, and women and perfume, all mixed in together. And there was more besides. There was sewage, grease, and commerce too. It was a strange and confusing scent, and one Chase really wasn't overly keen on.

It suffocated him. He tried then, unsuccessfully, to stifle a wide yawn. At that very moment, Black suddenly swerved.

The hard crack of a rifle shot split through the darkening silence.

A bullet passed so close to Chase's face that he felt the breeze on his cheek. For the second time that night, the black horse reared high, pawing at the air, snorting in fear. This time, Chase threw himself out of the saddle, without conscious thought. As he hit the ground, he instinctively curled into as small a ball as he could, and was quickly rolling towards the closest cover, and drawing his Colt.

From the corner of his eye, he'd seen Black take off at full speed into the darkness. He knew the horse was fine, he'd be safe, and he'd be back, either when his master called him, or when he knew the trouble was over. Chase dived behind a ragged pile of rocks, as another shot rang out. It thudded deep into the ground beside him, leaving a fountain of dust and a crater in its wake.

It was close. Too damned close for comfort.

The bushwhacker had a pretty good bead on him. Chase

hadn't been able to pinpoint his attacker's position in the gathering gloom. All he could tell, and not with any great certainty, was the rough direction the shots were coming from.

Slowly, cautiously, he eased himself forward, low on his elbows, into a place from where he could peer around the boulders fairly safely. As he moved, another two shots cracked loudly on the rocks in rapid succession, echoing through the arroyo, and sending a shower of shards and dust high into the darkening air. Close enough to cover him with debris. Chase ducked, looked around him, and silently cursed his position. He didn't dare try a shot from here; it would pinpoint his position and give the other man a sitting target to aim at.

On this side of the wash there was no more cover left, it had already petered out, mostly to rough plain. His assailant should have waited just a minute or two more, Chase thought grimly; there was no more cover now between here and Poynter, and as soon as Chase had left the arroyo the sniper would have had a clean shot. He'd have had a clean back-shot.

Any bounty hunter would have seen that; anyone who was out for a kill of any sort would have done better to wait just a few moments longer. His assailant was a pretty good shot, but Chase reckoned he was just an amateur. Any professional gunslinger would never have missed with those two shots. The other side of the arroyo was still fairly steep, covered with small and stunted bushes, and sagebrush, loose scree, and assorted boulders, many of them large enough though to act as cover for an ambush.

Without being able to pinpoint his attacker in the gloom, and with no other cover close by to move to, Chase was trapped. It was getting dark pretty fast now, and the moon was only a thin sickle in the now almost black sky. The light from the stars wasn't enough to really see much by.

Soon there wouldn't be enough of any kind of light to get off any good shots, so Chase figured that either the hidden sniper had eyes that could see in the dark, or else he'd soon be leaving. Moments later, his hunch proved right, when he heard a horse galloping away from the rocks. Quickly moving forward, and kneeling, to keep as a low a target as possible, he could just about make out the shape of the horse, and its rider, hunkered down real close to his mount's neck, to present as small a target as possible.

They were moving fast, too far away now for him to get a good shot with a handgun, and Black, wherever he'd run off to, still had the Winchester strapped to his saddle. Chase hadn't thought he'd need to be so well-armed, this close to the place he still called home.

He swore loudly as he stood up cautiously, and peered out through the gloom at the back of his assailant, who was fast disappearing like a ghost in the night. He too, it seemed, was heading in the general direction of Poynter. Did Chase know him? Or had it been just a chance encounter? The hairs on the back of his neck prickled, warning him; he'd learned over the years to listen to those warnings.

Chance encounter? The hell it was!

Someone, somehow, had known he was coming; they'd known when he'd be here, and they'd known exactly the road that he'd be taking. For some reason, someone was trying to stop him reaching the town. It looked as though a different sort of sidewinder was out to cause trouble now.

He whistled long and low, and was quickly answered by a soft whinny. Black trotted out of the darkness towards him, unhurt, prancing, tossing his head, and snorting. Mounting quickly, Chase urged the stallion on. Maybe they'd be able to get into town fast enough to find out just who it was who'd been taking pot shots at him in the darkness. And who it was who wanted to keep him out of the town. He had one hell of a damn good idea.

Black carried him swiftly onwards, sensing the urgent need for more speed now. Chase had lost sight of his attacker in the gathering darkness, but he knew the only place he could feasibly be heading for was Poynter. There was no other town for miles around. There were hardly any homesteads this side of town for the sidewinder to slither off to, like the snake that he was, either. There were a few scattered small homesteads the other side of town. Maybe he'd headed for one of them. No chance of finding the bastard now.

Chase had always kept his nose clean around here. His sister and her children meant a hell of a lot to him, and he'd do nothing to cause them any worries, so he couldn't, for the life of him, figure out just why anyone hereabouts would want to take a shot at him.

Except Bill perhaps, and he'd be just plain stupid to risk a damn fool trick like this, so close to home. Chase knew very well, though, that Bill wasn't mule stupid; he might be an awful lot of things, but stupid certainly wasn't one of them.

His brother-in-law was a good deal more intelligent than he liked to let on, and Chase had seen through his act of mild mannered storekeeper right away. There was a hell of a lot going on under that gunnysack apron and slicked back, thinning, brown hair. The false smile he pasted on for the benefit of his customers really didn't fool Chase in any way.

Bill could very easily have paid someone else to do the job for him; he was as sneaky as an old coyote, and not past bribing some drifter down on his luck to carry out a killing for him. That could explain why the shots missed; they'd been fired by an amateur.

Chase had wired Annelise from Coyote Springs, the last town he'd stopped in; they'd know the travelling time from there, so they'd know he'd be arriving around now. Trouble with wires was, anyone else who was around the telegraph office when they went out, or came in, would also know he was coming, and not all of the employees were as tight-mouthed as they should be about some of the messages they read. And most men could be bought.

Of course, he knew he couldn't just come right out and accuse his brother-in-law, not without any real, solid proof. But all the while he was back here in Poynter Chase knew now that he'd have to be on his guard. He usually was when he was around Bill anyway, but no one here had tried to kill him before. He reckoned he'd have to be extra wary this time round.

Black slowed his pace down to a measured trot; they were at the outskirts of the town now.

'Walk steady, boy,' said Chase, as he let the reins lie loose on Black's neck.

Black immediately eased down into a leisurely walk, letting his head drop level with his shoulders, easing the travel tension out of his neck muscles, and taking his time ambling down the centre of the town's main street. He knew, from past times visiting the place, just exactly where he should be headed.

Poynter had grown up around a couple of the bigger homesteads, and had developed into quite a popular little township. It sported three saloons, one with a good livery attached; a small cat house; a number of small stores, and a Chinese laundry and a bathhouse. There was a staging post, a telegraph office, a sheriff's office, and a large trading post and general store, which was run by Chase's sister and her husband.

It was quiet now: this late at night there was only an occasional rider walking his horse slowly along the street, or small groups of people hanging about. The saloons were busy already, of course, but it was still pretty early, nobody had gotten drunk enough to be thrown out on to the side walk just yet.

Chase's eyes quickly scanned each side of the road. He was looking for a horse in a lather, whilst at the same time not really expecting to find one. Whoever had tried to kill him, if they'd any sense at all, would have hidden their animal away by now. There was no point in running over to the sheriff's office to tell him about the attack, there'd be a whole heap of paperwork to fill in, and anyway there was no real proof, only his word, so Chase decided he was going to keep his mouth shut, for now anyway.

Black stopped outside the Dime and Nugget hotel, one of the better places, on the outer edge of the town, not usually frequented by the 'good-time girls' and fighters. The front of the hotel was in need of a good lick of paint, and the sign hung askew on its post, but they'd used it before, and Chase knew that, despite outward appearances, it was clean and quiet.

He also knew they had a livery here, as good as any he'd used anywhere; it was important to him that Black was well looked after. Chase wouldn't sleep at his sister's house whilst he was in town; never did. He really didn't want to be under the same roof as Bill in the dead of night; he never knew what sort of sneaky tricks his brother-in-law might get up to. It had upset Annelise at first, but she'd reluctantly gotten used to the arrangement by now.

As Black halted out front of the building, a small, skinny,

barefoot boy in threadbare clothes, near enough a size too small for him, jumped up from the front steps.

'Take yuh hoss, mister?'

His dirty face looked eagerly up at Chase, who glanced quickly around the street again, just in case there was a sweated-up horse tied anywhere. He looked down at the boy. He guessed him to be about nine or ten years of age.

'You seen anyone else ride into town tonight, son?'

The boy shook his head immediately, untidy, greasy brown hair flopping around his big bright eyes; he wasn't lying.

'No sir, I been sittin' out here since noon, you're the first stranger I seed today.'

Chase took that comment to mean that, anyone else who had ridden in tonight must have been known to the boy. He rephrased the question carefully, just to be certain.

'Anyone else ride in tonight on the same trail as me, son? Maybe someone in a hurry, anyone from hereabouts, maybe?'

'Not as I've seed, mister.'

Chase swung down from the saddle and stretched, straightening out the kinks from his spine, and patted Black's muscular, dusty, neck.

'It's OK, kid; I'll see to the horse myself.'

'Please, mister?'

The child looked plaintively up at him, wide eyes shining eagerly. Chase smiled down at the dirty-faced little urchin. Something about him made Chase think of his nephew, Charlie.

'Well, I guess you can come along and fetch and carry for me if you like, son.'

'Thanks, mister!'

The boy made a grab for Black's reins before Chase could

warn him off, and the horse shied noisily away, dropping back on his hocks, half-rearing, eyes rolling, nostrils flaring, and snorting like a dragon. Black wouldn't allow any other rider to top him. He'd turn into a firebrand of the first order if ever that happened. He'd behave like a completely unbroken mustang. Unless, that is, Chase told him it was OK. Then he'd behave like an overfed and docile carthorse. However, those times were pretty rare.

Now he stood, still snorting gently, showing the whites of his eyes, and baring his teeth in what looked to the kid remarkably like a snarl. The boy had jumped quickly back, his eyes as wide as a coney on the run. Chase quickly had to stifle a smile at the look on the lad's face.

'It's OK, kid, he won't let nobody else touch him, less'n I tell him it's right.'

The boy smiled crookedly, shaking his head in disbelief.

'Nah, ain't no hoss understands man talk.'

He shook his head, looking warily up at Black, who now stood as quietly as a statue, large, expressive, brown eyes fixed squarely on the boy, nostrils flaring to pick up his scent, ears moving every which way.

'True, just watch.'

Chase stroked the horse's muzzle gently,

'Black, the kid's OK, old fella. Let him take you in.'

He turned and smiled down at the boy,

'It's fine now, son. Take hold of the reins, but don't make a sudden grab for 'em.'

Warily then, the boy reached his hand out. He couldn't quite reach the reins, and seemed afraid now to get too close to Black, who, it appeared, was sizing up the situation. Then the horse slowly took a step forward, lowering his head towards the boy, so that the reins were hanging just within his reach. The boy took hold of them tentatively, and turned, walking slowly down the side of the hotel to the stables, with Black following closely at his heels like a large, docile, dog.

The boy was grinning widely as he led the horse into a free stall. There were two other horses in residence; they looked up as the small group entered, but soon lost interest, and went back to their hay racks. They both looked rested and comfortable.

Chase and the kid, who'd volunteered that his name was Petey, and whom Chase quickly liked enough to allow him to use his given name, rather than just 'mister', busied themselves with unsaddling and settling Black in, grooming, feeding, and watering him. Chase didn't go looking for the stable manager; he'd pay in the morning. He knew from the past that this livery was OK with that arrangement.

'There's not many *hombre*'s treat their hosses like you do, mist . . . Chase.'

Petey smiled up at him as the tall, muscular man stroked the now gleaming neck of his horse, and whispered into its ear. There was a tenderness in that touch that Petey didn't often see from the usual drifters he fetched and carried for.

'No? You watch how men treat their horses then, do you, kid?'

'Yeah, all the time, most of 'em, they just leave their animals tied up to the hitch rail, and go in for some booze. When they do that, I fetch some water and hay out for the hosses.'

'Good lad.' Chase ruffled Petey's lank hair. 'You keep right on doin' that, son. A man's horse is as important as his gun out here, ain't that right?'

'Yessir!' The boy grinned widely up at the man. Chase tossed him a coin. He caught it deftly, rubbed it with his grubby sleeve, and thrust it deep into a pocket.

'Thanks, mis . . . Chase.'

'OK kid, I'm turning in. You'd best be off to your home now, son. See ya.'

He picked up his roll and packs and headed towards the hotel. Petey watched him go, then headed back into the darkness of the stable. The warm, musky perfume of drowsy horse, sweet hay, linseed and leather, made the livery a comfortable place to sleep. He'd spent many a night there instead of going home.

Petey turned himself up a small pile of clean straw, in the corner nearest to Black's stall. He'd found himself an old horse blanket and, pulling it tightly around him, he curled up like a little dog, nestling down into the straw and munching on a strip of jerky that he'd pulled from one of his ragged pockets.

As he chewed on his meagre supper he smiled to himself. He was warm and safe, there was money in his pocket, and he'd made himself a new friend: a very special friend. His smile broadened at the thought.

CHAPTER FOUR

No one looked up when Chase entered the hotel; they were well used to strangers passing through. A tall *hombre* in dusty trail clothes caused no stir around here.

A small thin man, with slicked-back hair, and a thick, yellow moustache, with a dark stub of cigarette hanging from thin lips, was attempting to play an out of tune, beat-up old piano in a corner. A couple of primping dancing girls, in flouncy, brightly coloured dresses, and wearing too much make-up, were standing together beside him, and a few small groups of men, of various ages, were dotted around the tables with their drinks, some playing cards, others just talking.

The girls gazed across at Chase with more than just a little thinly disguised interest. A tall, broad, good-looking stranger was something to take a real good look at. But he showed no interest in return: he was far too tired even to think about women tonight.

He dropped his packs beside him when he reached the counter. The desk clerk looked up, Chase didn't recognize him. The clerk was a balding, plump, greasy-looking little man, with hair so slicked with pomade that it looked as if it was painted on to his skull, and whose sweaty, white shirt almost matched the pallor of his flesh. He had an arrogant gleam in his watery pale-blue eyes, which made Chase bristle before the man even spoke.

'How long?' the clerk asked curtly, not even looking up at Chase.

'Coupl'a days, maybe more. Depends.'

The clerk scribbled something on to a page of the thick, leather-bound register. He turned it round, handed Chase the pen, and pushed the register towards him.

'Two days. Make yer mark.'

He spat a wad of chewing tobacco down into a handy spittoon, still not looking at Chase, who felt his hackles rising dangerously at the casual and ignorant attitude of the little clerk.

Chase signed his name in the register with a flourish, pushing the book sharply back at the man, who, without even a glance at the page, simply turned, took a key from the rail on the wall behind him, and threw it casually on to the counter. He grabbed up the coins Chase had tossed on the counter, and thrust them into a box beneath it.

'Room 11, mister. Upstairs, and to the back.'

He jerked his thumb in the general direction of the stairs and then began shuffling through the papers on the desk. He was still pointedly not looking at Chase, who angrily swept up the key, picked up his belongings, and sauntered over to the stairs. He looked around curiously as he went, taking in the faces seated around the place.

None of them looked as if they'd only just ridden in. That confirmed his suspicions; whoever had taken that shot at him must live here, or pretty close by, and must have his own barn or stable where he could take his sweating animal directly.

Room number 11 was sparsely furnished and small, but

reasonably clean. Chase dropped his gear in the corner, pulled off his Stetson, and threw it on to the small dresser. Then he dropped on to the none too soft but clean-looking, bed. He passed a hand across his face, and ran it through his dark curls. His thick hair felt gritty; it and his beard were too long, and he'd come up against skunks that had smelled sweeter than the way he was smelling right now. He sat up again, and undid his saddle-bags and took out his money poke and a clean shirt.

He'd get over to the bathhouse, have himself a good shave and a hot bath, grab a meal and a shot of whiskey, then turn in for a good night's shut-eye before going over to see his sister in the morning. The hotel was still pretty quiet as he passed through the lobby, ignoring the leering glances of the painted dancing girls, and headed across the wide dirt street to the bathhouse.

He was warmly greeted by the owner, Mrs Phelps, a small, plump woman, dressed from head to toe in black, with yellow hair like straw, which was piled in a high and untidy heap on top of her head.

She had small brown eyes, and a glowing red face, which owed far more to her familiarity with the gin bottle than to any imported rouge powder. She kept said bottle close beside her person, and was often to be seen taking a long swig of the contents. Recognition gleamed in her bloodshot eyes as she spotted him walking in. She searched deep in her brain for his name. She prided herself in always being able to remember a client's name, even after quite a long absence.

'Howdy, Mr – er – oh, now, let me think: Mr Tyler isn't it? Good t'see yuh agin; it's bin a long time. Hot tub, is it?'

'Howdy, Mrs Phelps. Yeah, that sounds real good. You still got that little Chinese cut-throat workin' for you?'

He smiled down at her.

'Mr Chung? Sure have. Book yuh in for a shave with him, will I?'

'Yeah, he gives one of the best shaves I've ever had, and I reckon I'll have me a bath after.'

Mrs Phelps licked the end of a stub of pencil and scribbled in a thin red book.

'Right then, room three's empty. Mr Chung will see to you just as soon as he's free.'

Chase strolled across to the room indicated, and went in. A small fire smouldered in the hearth, and a basket of logs stood ready to top it up if needed; even in the summer a man could get a chill sitting around damp from his bath.

The small room contained a large, roll-topped china bath on ball-and-claw feet. A long wooden bench seat filled one wall, and a line of old brass hooks for clothes was positioned above it. Chase unrolled his clean shirt and hung it on one of the hooks.

The carpet was stained and more than a little threadbare; a tattered and rather lumpy leather wing-back armchair stood close to the fire. A large boot-jack stood close by.

In front of the window a solid wooden upright chair, which had seen better days, had been placed at a desk, which was well supplied with writing paper, pens and ink, a box of assorted cigars with a cutter, and a box of lucifers.

The clientele of this establishment were not the usual drifters and drunkards; they had a bit more taste, and certainly a deal more money. Mostly they were passengers from the stage. Usually men with money rode the stages, men who were a little more particular about their appearance than the drifters. And Chase, though technically a drifter, liked to maintain a certain pride in his appearance; he hadn't yet reached the stage of wild unkempt hair and beard, and too much whiskey.

In one corner of the room, near the window, to allow for good light for shaving, stood a large, worn leather barber chair, with a wooden washstand close by, holding a bowl, towel, block of rough brown soap, and a large pitcher of cold water.

Chase took off his Stetson, banged it against his legs to loosen the dust, and placed it on one of the brass hooks. He shrugged off his jacket, dusted it down with a couple of swipes of his hand, and hung it on another of the hooks. Crossing to the window, he took a look outside. The room was at the rear of the bathhouse; close on the last place in town; the area behind it was empty of people, and the only view was that of the back of another building.

He went over to the armchair, took off his gunbelt, rolled it, and placed it on the floor in arm's reach of the chair. He sat and pulled the boot-jack towards him, prising off his dusty boots, then leaned right back in the chair and stretched, catlike, from the tips of his fingers to the tips of his toes, straightening out his spine, and easing each and every muscle of his slim, broad-shouldered, frame.

He sighed a deep and contented sigh, he was warm and fairly comfortable now, soon he'd be clean, and clean-shaven, and a good night's sleep in a proper bed, instead of on the ground, would ensure he was bright-eyed and bushy-tailed in the morning.

A gentle knock on the door brought Chase back down to earth. The door opened and a small, plump, Chinese man entered. He wore black trousers and shoes, and a beautifully embroidered, vivid blue silk tunic. A red-and-black embroidered skullcap was perched neatly over his tightly plaited, shiny black hair.

The Chinaman was carrying an ornately carved wooden

box, and had a large pile of towels over his arm. He bowed as low as his burden would allow, as he stood in the doorway.

'Mr Tyler, sir, welcome to our humble establishment once more. Mrs Phelps say you want close shave?'

'I've already had one of them thanks.' Chase laughed, then he saw the puzzled look on Mr Chung's face.

'Yeah, one of your special shaves please. Nothing like it anywhere else I've been. Nice to see you again, Mr Chung. Family doin' well, are they?'

Mr Chung busied himself with laying the towels out on the shelf, getting his shaving equipment out of the box, and setting it out methodically on the washstand.

'Thank you for asking, Mr Tyler. Yes, they are very well. I have two children now, one boy, one small girl. They are very good children. We are very truly blessed.'

He began to sharpen the large cut-throat razor on the wide, well-used strop that he had taken from the box.

'We wait now for hot water only, Mr Tyler; it will be here shortly. Mrs Phelps say the boiler for your bath is now on; it will be ready for you very soon.'

He turned and bowed to Chase, then stood rigidly, arms folded, hands tucked deeply into his shiny blue sleeves, looking at Chase's face, weighing up the contours, planes, and hollows, deciding how best to do his work.

'Mr Chung, please sit yourself down while we wait, it's fine if you do, really.'

Chase motioned towards the bench where Mr Chung had placed the towels. The Chinaman shook his head, the stiff black braid swishing across his blue silk back.

'I am here now for business, Mr Tyler, not for sitting, thank you.'

There was a light rapping at the door; Mr Chung opened it at once. A pretty, young blonde girl stood there, with a tray containing a pitcher and a bowl of steaming, scented, hot water, in which a clean, folded, towel lay soaking, ready to be placed on Chase's face after the shave.

She looked past the Chinaman, at the broad-shouldered, long-legged man stretched out in the armchair. She smiled over at him, even though he wasn't looking. Mr Chung took the tray from the girl and gave her as deep a bow as the pitcher would allow without spilling. She returned his bow with a fond smile, turned, and left. Mr Chung shut the door and turned to Chase, who was relaxing in the chair, legs straight out in front of him, hands folded behind his head, eyes closed.

'Mr Tyler, shave is ready now.'

Chase stretched, stifled a yawn, stood, and crossed over to the barber chair. At the same time Mr Chung, crossing to get another towel, moved over and got in his way. Chase paused, Mr Chung paused, then they both moved together, in the same direction, and bumped into one another. They vied for position then, with friendly smiles.

'OK, Mr Chung, you go that way, I'll go this way.' Chase indicated. 'Then I can sit, and you can shave, how's that?'

Mr Chung bowed. They both moved at once and in that very same instant a loud shot rang out. The window shattered, propelling a shower of glass splinters right across the room. Chase launched himself at the Chinaman, knocking him to the floor with his shoulder. At almost the same time he grabbed up his gunbelt, flipped it out to unroll it, and yanked the Colt free of the holster. Down on the floor, he propelled himself over towards the window.

The broken shards of glass crunched on the carpet beneath him as he rolled across it, ending up crouching close beside the window. He peered cautiously over the ledge as another shot rang out, winging loudly past his ear,

47

causing him to duck low behind the window frame.

He quickly reckoned the direction from which the shot had come: the corner of the building opposite. He'd figured now that it was the back of the livery stable. He couldn't see any movements from that direction though; the night was dark and the moon was weak, a perfect night for the miserable coyote to hide himself in.

'Mr Chung,' Chase whispered. The little man should get out of the room real quick, it wasn't safe for him to be in here right now.

'Mr Chung?'

There was no answer. Chase turned; the little Chinese man was lying spread-eagled, close by the washstand, a ruby pool of dark blood spreading ominously across the beautifully vivid blue silk of his chest.

'Oh shit! No!'

Chase turned back to the window; still he could see nothing moving. The door behind him crashed open, Chase swung himself round, gun cocked, finger on the trigger ready to fire. Luckily though, he didn't let off a shot.

'Mrs Phelps! For God's sake get out – and close the door.'

The woman had taken in the sight of Mr Chung's lifeless body, and the gun in Chase's hand. As she retreated, eyes wide with fear, shutting the door quickly, another shot thudded into the window frame, going deep, and splintering the wood. Chase sat back down on the floor beside the window, listening carefully. There was no sound from outside the building now, and somehow he suddenly knew, with senses honed sharp by years on the trail, that his assailant had left. It had to be the same damned varmint that had tried to bushwhack him earlier. Only now they'd killed a completely innocent man.

Chase glanced across at Mr Chung again; by now, the ugly

red stain was spreading across the rug. There was no doubt at all that the little man was dead. Chase was real angry now.

When he found out who was responsible, he'd kill them – after he'd taken a very slow, and painful, revenge for Mr Chung. Chase stood up; he knew there'd be no more shots now. Quickly, he pulled on his boots, and buckled on his gunbelt, then went out to talk to Mrs Phelps. She was sitting at a table in the lobby of the bathhouse, drinking from her half-empty bottle of gin, taking deep swigs, and swiping at her mouth with the back of her hand. She looked up at his approach, her eyes wide, her pale face whiter than usual, her scarlet lipstick spread in a bright smudge over her cheek where she'd wiped her hand across her mouth.

'My God, Mr Tyler, why in the name of all the devils in hell would anybody ever want to kill poor Mr Chung? The sheriff's on his way.'

That much should have been obvious. Late though it was, the noise of the shots must have caused some waves in the normally peaceful town; the sheriff was duty bound to leave the comfort of his office, or more likely, his bed, and investigate.

Mrs Phelps placed the half-empty gin bottle nervously on the table beside her, shaking her head in stark disbelief. The movement caused strands of her untidy yellow hair to come undone and tumble down round her florid face.

'They wanted me, Mrs Phelps, me, not Mr Chung. He just got in the way of the bullet, the poor little beggar.'

'But what am I going to tell his family? He's got a lovely wife, and two little'uns.'

She wrung her pudgy pale hands together in despair, and fat tears rolled freely down her plump cheeks. Chase took the pouch from his pocket, and emptied a pile of notes and coins on to the desk, holding back just enough to last him a

49

couple of days.

'It won't make up for their loss, I know that, but it might help ease their way, just a little.'

Mrs Phelps took hold of his rough hand between her own soft, warm ones.

'Mr Tyler, Chase, you truly are a wonderful, wonderful man. I hope you catch up with that bushwhackin' sonofabitch, and when you do, you kill him real slow, for the Chinaman.'

She picked up the bottle, frowned deeply, and waved it at Chase like a weapon, then took another long swig from the nearly empty vessel. Just then the sheriff burst in, causing her to leap with fright, and spill most of what was left of the contents of the bottle down her blouse front. She attempted to wipe it away; the sweet, perfumed smell of the gin pervaded the room.

'Oh, my poor heart! I thought you was the gunslinger. This here is Mr Tyler. He's OK. It wasn't him as killed poor Mr Chung, he was just here for a shave. His family own Murdoch's store.'

She called out to Jim, the old man who did the odd jobs and cleaning around the place, explaining what she wanted him to do. Then she called up one of her girls, and told her to run over to the undertaker's. Sighing deeply, Mrs Phelps then disappeared into her small office, preparing herself to be the bearer of the worst kind of news. She was clutching the money Chase had given her in one hand, and the almost empty bottle in the other, as if it was a life preserver.

The sheriff looked Chase up and down curiously. Chase returned his gaze unflinchingly. The sheriff was a stout, short, grey-haired feller, only just the right side of sixty, Chase guessed. His was a face Chase didn't recognize. He seemed like the sort of *hombre* who spent most of his time sitting safely behind his desk, only coming out to show off his badge when it seemed the right thing to do.

It appeared to Chase as if the sheriff had hardly ever ridden a horse, or fired off a gun in anger, relying on the fact that the town had always been a peaceable one, to keep his office. He wore his gunbelt high, tight, and obviously uncomfortably. It looked to Chase's eyes as if it were almost new, and only worn on special occasions.

The sheriff nodded to Chase, introducing himself as Sheriff Mike Thomas; he'd been coming over to take Chase in for questioning. It was just a formality though, as he'd already had a quick word with everyone else who'd been there and all of their stories tallied up. Chase couldn't have killed the Chinaman.

All thoughts of baths and shaves long since gone, Chase went back in to the shaving room to fetch his belongings. The old man had placed a sheet over the body of Mr Chung, and was busying himself sweeping and picking up the shards of shattered glass. He didn't even look up as Chase picked up his things.

Chase went across to the jailhouse with the sheriff to give him his own statement of the night's events. As they left the bathhouse, the sheriff cleared away the few citizens who were curiously standing around, waiting to find out what had caused the commotion.

At the sheriff's office Chase told his tale, leaving out the shooting in the arroyo; he didn't want to complicate matters any further. After writing the statement out and getting Chase to put his signature to it, the sheriff sat back in his chair and leaned his elbows on his desk, steepling his fingers in front of him and staring across at the younger man.

'Well, I reckon it's gonna be hard to find out who the perpetrator was, Mr Tyler. No one saw anybody. Might as well

have been a ghost for all I can find out. But I'll be keepin'
my ear to the ground. If'n I do find anything out, I'll be sure
to let you know. But you leave it to me now, Mr Tyler, don't
you go tryin' to take the law into your own hands; do y'hear
what I'm sayin'?'

Sheriff Thomas frowned up at the younger man. He had
sized Chase up and got his full measure all right. He could
see that the other man was way more than capable of
looking after himself, but he was the law here, and it really
wouldn't do to have every newcomer feudin' and fightin' all
over the place.

Chase had met the sheriff's kind before, all wind and
show, no real teeth, but he allowed the older man to believe
he'd leave the investigating up to him; it wouldn't do any
harm.

He didn't believe there would be any real investigation
going on anyways. After all, he was a stranger here, to all
intents and purposes. The sheriff's real duty was to his resi-
dent citizens: he wouldn't bother chasing up an isolated
incident against a drifter. He wouldn't think it was worth his
time or effort, not when Chase would most probably be gone
in a day or so anyway.

That Mr Chung had been killed was certainly a tragic
event, but it was obvious the shooter hadn't been aiming for
the little man; it was simply an awful accident. There was no
need for any sort of investigation on that score at least.

Well, that was fine by Chase; it meant the old man would-
n't be getting in his way. Sheriff Thomas was a guy who was
far more comfortable riding his desk. Chase told the sheriff
where he would be lodging, and headed back across to his
room. He went to the stables first, though; he needed to
check on Black and little Petey. He hoped the skunk who'd
killed Mr Chung hadn't harmed the boy. The shots had

come from the area around the livery, right where he'd left the boy earlier, alone.

Chase entered the stables cautiously, hand close to his gun, nerves wound up real tight, and ready to shoot if there was anything wrong. Black whickered a soft greeting; he was OK, but where was Petey? There was no sign of the boy. Chase quietly called out his name. There was no answer.

He looked around the place, and quickly took in the nest of straw, and the tattered blanket that the boy had settled down in earlier; it was empty. He reckoned the kid must have a home to go to, and wasn't bedding down in the livery permanently. He just hoped that the kid was around, and unharmed, or there might well be two murders to be avenged. He was plenty angry now, and plenty ready to avenge them.

It was well past dark; the kid could be anywhere by now. Chase would look for him in the morning, there was nothing more that anyone could do tonight. Feeding a handful of mash to Black, Chase wondered what was going on here. Someone sure as hell didn't want him around. He'd have to be on his guard all the while he was in town now.

He stopped off for a quick shot of whiskey on the way up to his room, and spotted the desk clerk watching him closely, all the while pretending to shuffle the papers on his counter. That *hombre* was a two-faced one if ever there was; maybe it was him that had tried for Chase. But no, that didn't make any sense; the clerk had already been in here when he arrived. Chase knew he really had to get some rest, he was seeing murderers everywhere, and it didn't do to go getting too nervy. That way you'd miss the important clues.

He had ordered a pitcher of hot water and a block of soap to be sent up to his room. When they came he took off his dirty clothes and had himself a good strip-down wash and a shave; not as good as the one he'd have had from poor Mr Chung, but it'd have to do.

His body was sun-tanned and lean, with not an ounce of spare fat; well-defined muscles rippled beneath taut, healthy skin. A few white scars, of various sizes, were peppered around his body, and shone out from the rest of his flesh; every one of them had a tale to tell. Every one of them had served to make Chase Tyler the man he was today.

The bed was hard, but it was fairly comfortable; the hotel was comparatively quiet. It didn't take him very long to get off to sleep, his gun close beside him under the pillow, just in case the varmint tried to get him in his unguarded moments.

Although he slept well, all his keenly-honed senses were constantly on the alert for any sound. Even the scampering of a mouse didn't escape his half-sleeping mind. Should anyone have entered his room, he'd have been ready to defend himself in an instant.

Someone was out to get him, and as yet he didn't know who it was, or why. He had a ghost of an idea, and he'd sure find out, one way or another.

He was more tired than he'd thought. He slept well, but fitfully, and he dreamed. He didn't often dream. He was usually too on edge to have dreams. But this night, for some reason, perhaps because of where he was, the dreams came to him. They were all of a red-haired, freckle-faced teenage girl, with eyes as green as a spring meadow, and a smile he would have died for.

In his restless sleep, he whispered her name.

'Jess.'

CHAPTER FIVE

The following morning, well rested, in a clean shirt, and after a good breakfast at the hotel, Chase went on over to the livery to check on Black. Petey still wasn't around, but there was a wizened old-timer watering the horses. He nodded as he saw Chase enter.

'Howdy there, stranger.'

'Howdy. Just checkin' on my horse here. Say, where's the kid, Petey, this morning?'

The old-timer shook his head and spat into the dust.

'Dunno. He wasn't here when I got in. He's mostly in before me; still, he lives by his own rules that one. Be around later I don't doubt.'

Chase hoped so; he didn't want to think of any harm coming to the lad. He fed and watered Black, and as the stallion was eating he went round and checked him out carefully, as was his usual routine. He lifted each leg in turn, checking feet, shoes, fetlocks and hocks, and running his hands expertly over the animal's muscular body.

There appeared to be nothing untoward with the horse at least. Chase sighed with relief, Black turned and nuzzled at his master's back gently. Chase fed him an extra handful of oats, then, with one last friendly slap on Black's gleaming blue-black quarters, he headed off at last for his sister's place.

The Murdochs' store sold general merchandise, food, hardware, traps, ropes, chains and such: most things that anyone might need, in fact, and, from the look of it, the family were doing real well. A lot better than Chase would have thought from a small-town store. It filled almost half a block now: the paintwork was neat and new, and the windows gleamed. Money had obviously been lavished on the place lately.

He mentally steeled himself for meeting Bill as he headed towards the store. The doorbell jangled harshly as he pushed the door open and went in. The smell surrounded him; it was a mixture of all the things on sale in the shop, and of Annelise's cooking, the delicious aroma drifting through the half-closed door and infiltrating into the shop.

Bill was up on a ladder, stocking the shelves with tins and packets, with his back to the door. He turned as he heard the bell, a pasted-on smile across his face. When he saw that the customer was only Chase, the false smile faded quicker than ice in the midsummer sun. Chase attempted to put on a cheery tone of voice, but it almost sounded, even to his own ears, like a snarl.

'Howdy Bill, Annelise out back?'

'Sure,' was the gruff reply, as Bill turned back and carried on stocking the shelves.

Chase carried on through the store, and out to the back living area, where a little boy and girl were chasing each other round and round the furniture, and giggling loudly. He could see Annelise, she was busy at the oven, and he glimpsed the corner of the small pen where he reckoned little Susie would be playing.

The boy ran into the man's legs, and staggered backwards

to sit down hard on the floor.

'Sorry, mister,' he gasped with a breathless giggle, looking upwards as his sister came to a sudden stop by running right into his back, almost falling over her brother.

Sudden recognition lit up his wide blue eyes.

'Uncle Chase! Ma! Ma! It's Uncle Chase!'

Annelise hurried in from the outer kitchen, wiping her hands on her apron, and rushed over to him.

'Chase, you're OK. Oh thank God.'

She flung her arms around him and the two children jumped up and down then clung to his legs like limpets, both of them chattering away excitedly. Even when his sister had let go of him for long enough to go and put the pot of coffee on the stove, the kids still hung on to him.

He suddenly felt a bit hemmed in, suffocated; it was a feeling he wasn't too keen on. Sure, he had a certain feeling for his sister's youngsters, but all that noise and hanging on was a bit too much for a loner like him.

'OK, OK, you two, let me go now, so I can breathe. Let's go sit ourselves down some place, then you can tell me what you've all been up to since my last visit. I'll bet you've got lots of exciting things to tell me, eh?'

He herded them along in front of him to the kitchen, where the delicious smell of cinnamon cookies baking filled the air. He sat at the large table and looked around him as the children clambered up on to their chairs. The place had grown a hell of a lot since he was here last, it must be doing well; this was a much newer, much bigger kitchen. He watched absently as his sister pulled another batch of cookies from the oven and laid them on the cooling racks.

The kids had grown a heap too. He never ceased to be amazed by just how quickly all young animals grew. Annelise poured him out a steaming mug of thick black coffee.

'Thanks, Sis. OK, now then, let's hear it all. How's everything hereabouts?'

Annelise was a striking-looking woman, almost as tall as her brother; still retaining her slim figure despite having had four children. She was strong, curvaceous, and the grace of the dancer she'd once wanted to be showed in her every movement as she busied herself at the stove.

She brushed the long dark curls back from her eyes and sat down opposite him, searching his face with her eager blue gaze, and clutching her own coffee in both hands, although she wasn't about to ask what he'd been up to. All too often, with her brother, she'd learned it was probably a heck of a lot better not to know exactly what he'd been up to.

Her eyes were taking in every inch of his strong face, as if searching for the answers to many unspoken questions. Charlie and Mary knelt up at the table, wriggling excitedly at the thought of the tales to come.

'Uncle Chase, tell us a story, please,' pleaded Mary sweetly, her big blue eyes, with long dark lashes, echoing both those of her mother and uncle.

'Yeah, Uncle Chase, tell us about them four cattle rustlers you hanged single handed.'

Charlie's eyes gleamed with the morbid delight of a fast-growing boy.

'Please!' Mary cried out eagerly, clapping her small hands, bright blue eyes sparkling.

'Pleeeease, Uncle Chase, a story?'

Charlie leaned forward, kneeling up on his chair in eager anticipation, and reaching his arms out across the table.

'Can I hold your gun, Uncle Chase. Please?'

'Children, give it up. Uncle Chase will tell you lots of stories later; just now, though, he wants to talk with me. He needs to catch up on all the news hereabouts. A lot of things have happened since he was here last, haven't they? And no, Charlie, you can't hold his gun.'

She glanced meaningfully over at Chase. 'Now you two go on out to the yard and play.'

She shooed them off out, amid groans of protest, passing them a freshly baked cinnamon cookie each as they rushed past her.

'There, that'll see you through till lunch. Careful, they're still warm.'

She handed down one of her cold, first batch of sweet cookies, to two-year-old Susie, who sat quietly in the corner of the pen, holding on to a small rag doll, and looking shyly up at her uncle. She was still too young to really remember seeing him before; he was a total stranger to her young eyes.

The new baby was sleeping peacefully in his cradle, beside the stove. Chase went over and looked down into the cradle, seeing just a round, pink, wrinkled face with a mop of dark hair and thick dark lashes resting on pale chubby cheeks. All babies looked the same to him; he couldn't really see the attraction himself.

'You've really got your hands full now, Sis.'

He took off his gun belt, rolled it, and placed it, safe out of the reach of the boy, on a shelf above the dresser, and went back to his seat at the table. The baby woke then, and whimpered quietly. Chase looked across at the new arrival.

'Oh, you know I love it, brother. Admitted, they do drive me plumb crazy sometimes, but I did always want a lot of kids, didn't I?'

'Yeah, I remember, you were always playin' make-believe with anything that was small enough to be picked up. You had some pretty strange children back in those days, Sis.'

They laughed loudly together at the memories.

'Yes, my children were chickens, piglets, dogs, cats, and sometimes even you, if I recall, but your own, real, children are so much more satisfying. I wish you. . . .'

Her voice tailed off as her brother looked away quickly, and she bit her lip, regretting what she'd been about to say.

'How are you all though, 'Lise?'

He was real serious now.

'I'm fine, Chase, honestly. Me and the kids, we want for nothing, and the business is doing great. Well, you can see that, can't you?'

She smiled broadly; it really looked as if she was happy. He looked around him.

'Yeah, it looks like it's doin' real fine, what about . . . Bill?'

His throat tightened as he said his brother-in-law's name; he felt almost as if he was going to choke on the word. Annelise didn't miss the catch in his voice, and smiled ruefully at her brother.

'Oh Chase! Bill's OK, you know he'd never do anything to harm any of us – not even you,' she added hastily. 'I really do wish you two would settle your differences. I'd have thought, after so long, you might at least be civil to one another.'

'Sorry, Sis, so long as he treats you all fair, well, that's OK, but just don't ask me to like the feller, that's all.'

Annelise saw the wry smile on her brother's lips, and knew he'd much rather see her married to someone else. Anyone else would do. Her husband and her brother had always hated one another, though she doubted if either of them could really explain why.

'Oh Chase, I heard about poor Mr Chung, what on earth happened? He was such a lovely man, and so good with the children, why the hell would anyone want to kill him?'

'Yeah, I was in there for a shave, He was telling me he had two little 'uns of his own now. Some buzzard wanted me though, 'Lise, not him; Mr Chung just got himself in the way of the bullet, that was all. It's a bloody goddamn shame.'

His sister instinctively raised a hand to her mouth to suppress a gasp of fear.

'Do you know who it was?'

'Most likely it was the same goddamn sonofabitch who took a pot shot at me on my way into town last night.'

'Someone's shot at you twice now? Why, Chase? Who?'

She looked around her nervously, frowning deeply, almost as if the perpetrator might be hiding in the house.

'Damned if I know, Sis; couldn't make him out. Whoever it was might just as well have been a ghost for all I could see of him. But when I get a hold of the bastard. . . .'

Annelise took hold of her brother's hand tightly and looked deeply into his sky-blue eyes.

'Oh Chase, be careful. If they've gone for you twice they're just as likely to try again, aren't they?'

'No, Sis, don't you worry. I've got his number. This sidewinder only strikes at night, under cover of darkness. I'm OK in the daylight, there's too many eyes about.'

'Did you tell the sheriff about that?'

'What's the point? I didn't see the guy, or even get a good look at his horse, it was way too dark. What do I tell the sheriff? "I was shot at by someone – who rode out to somewhere"? No, let's leave that one just between me and you, Sis. I reckon it's for the best if no one else knows.'

'Well, if you think so. But please, do be careful, Chase. Here, have a cookie.'

She pushed the tin across the table; he took a large handful of the sweet cinnamon cookies, and munched thoughtfully on them. Annelise smiled across at him. Still the little kid who could be tempted by a handful of cookies, despite some of the things she knew that he'd done in his life. She shook her head wistfully, remembering the carefree boy he once had been.

'Have there been any strangers around here lately, 'Lise? Anybody askin' 'bout me?'

'Not that I know of. Most folk end up calling in here for something, and we usually get to hear most of the gossip. There's been people moving in, and others leaving, as they will in any place, but no one asking for anyone in particular. Anyway, if they had wanted you, we'd have known, wouldn't we?'

'Guess so. Yeah.' He chewed thoughtfully on another cookie.

The baby started to cry. Annelise leaned into the cot and deftly changed his wet diaper. Then she picked him up and carried the mewling infant across, to sit with him in her rocking-chair near the table. As she settled herself down she began undoing her blouse to feed him. Chase averted his eyes, shifting uncomfortably in his chair.

'Didn't have you down as the bashful kind, brother.' Annelise smiled broadly.

Chase almost blushed beneath his tan.

'Well, hell, I'm not usually, but I'm kinda not used to seein' any decent woman's breasts up so close.'

'I'm not just any woman, Chase, I'm your sister.' She smiled.

Chase rose from his chair and headed for the door.

'Yeah and that makes it worse somehow. Tell you what, why don't I go find the young 'uns, chase 'em round a bit, tire 'em out for you?'

'Thanks. You're a real good uncle, Chase. I know you'll make a real good father one of these days. That is, if you can ever stay still long enough for some lucky girl to corral you.'

'Yeah, they're great kids, just like their ma, but I'm not

ready to be hobbled just yet, Sis. If ever now, I guess. I'll be back later, when I've worn 'em out for you.'

As the baby began feeding, with warm little snuffling grunts, Chase beat a hasty retreat, hurriedly going out back to find his nephew and niece.

He enjoyed the rare times he spent with the family, but really couldn't see himself setting up as a storekeeper; he valued his freedom too much, he was getting too set in his ways. At thirty, he reckoned he was a bit long in the tooth to be changing his life now.

He cared a great deal for his sister's children, and felt a really strong bond with them such as he'd seldom felt for many other living things. Except for Annelise herself, of course, and good old Black. And once . . . it seemed like so long ago now. Once there had been. . . .

Charlie charged at him, roaring like a young bull. Mary howled with laughter when Chase fell to the floor as if he was dead, and both the children leaped upon his prostrate body in delight.

He was soon lost in a rip-roaring rough-and-tumble around the yard with the children, which only ended when Annelise called them all in for lunch.

CHAPTER SIX

He felt himself tensing up as he entered the kitchen. Bill would be there, so he'd have to be polite. He looked around. Annelise, seeing his glances, smiled, and shook her head.

'Don't you worry yourself, little brother. Bill's had to go out to visit old Mr Barrow over at the Crooked Y, to deliver some groceries. You remember the place? It's a long drive out there; he won't be back much before dark.'

Chase relaxed; that was some sort of a coincidence. He wondered how urgent Mr Barrow's order was, or was it just an excuse for Bill to be out of his brother-in-law's way this time? If that was the case, well, Chase was more than happy enough with that arrangement.

Lunch was a delicious, if messy affair. The children all got stuck in to the meal like little pigs at a trough; it did Chase's heart good to see them tuck so much good food away, and he couldn't help his thoughts turning to Petey.

'Sis, you know a kid called Petey, skinny little thing, aged about ten or so I reckon, helps out at the livery?'

'Petey? Oh yes, he's a strange kid, that one; comes and goes; one day he's all over the place, next he's nowhere to be seen. Why?'

'No reason, just he seemed to be taken by old Black, feeding, grooming, talking to him, then he just wasn't there. What do you know about him?'

'Not a lot, really. Him and his big sister just seemed to appear in town one day, about a twelve-month or so back, I guess. Never really talk about where they came from.'

'Where does he go to? When he's not hangin' round town, I mean.'

'You know I'm not too sure, but they live out at the old Bar H place, you'll remember that, won't you? Next small spread north from the M? She keeps to herself mostly, and Petey comes and goes as he likes. He's a bit wild, but he's a really bright kid, earns himself a buck here and there doing odd jobs. He's excellent with the horses especially.'

'Yeah, I've seen him; he was real good with old Black. So he could be any place, then?'

'Sure, he flits around, whenever and wherever someone wants a job doing. He might only be a little 'un, but he's pretty strong, and he can turn his hand to most things. Why all the interest anyway, little brother? You worried about him or something?'

Chase had to admit to himself that, yes, he had indeed been worried. There'd been two recent attempts on his own life, an innocent family man had been killed because of him, and now the kid appeared to have gone missing. He reluctantly realized that he'd been afraid that whoever was out to get him might just try and do it through taking the kid. Maybe they'd thought Petey might have meant something to Chase, after watching them talking and working together.

He liked the kid for sure; certainly saw something in him, something he couldn't quite place. The last thing he wanted was for the boy to get hurt because some no-good sono-fabitch had made a mistake. Petey reminded Chase a bit of

Charlie – that was it, just a little bit older and wiser, and, strangely, Chase felt a similar kind of fondness for the kid as for his own nephew.

He decided he'd take a ride out to the Bar H and check on the kid, just to be sure. When he told Annelise of his plans she just smiled up at him, and shook her head slowly.

'That's really not a good idea, Chase. His sister – I think she's called Sarah? She won't tolerate any strangers anywhere near them. They've not got much of a spread out there, but what they do have she protects like a wildcat.'

'Yeah, but I'm not there to steal her land, am I, Sis? Just to check on the kid.'

His sister shook her head and opened her mouth to speak again, and just then the bell on the front door of the store jangled. Someone wanted waiting on, and she had to do it whenever her husband was away.

'Well, little brother, don't you dare come back here telling me that you weren't warned, when she tries to shoot your damn fool head off, then.'

She smiled up at him, shaking her head, and patted his arm gently as she headed past him for the shop door. Determined now to go and check on Petey, Chase buckled on his gunbelt, pushed his hat down over his black curls, and headed on over to the livery, glancing around as he did so, weighing up the other folk on the street. There didn't seem to be anyone acting in any ways out of the ordinary; one or two acknowledged him with a nod, or a touch to the rim of their hats, which he returned as he went on his way.

Some he recognized of old, others were strangers to him, but none made his senses prickle. He'd gotten used to that feeling that came over him whenever he came into contact with anyone who might mean trouble. And he listened to it. It had hardly ever let him down yet.

The livery was busy that morning. There was a lot of coming and going; all the stalls were full now. Chase went and found the livery manager, and handed over a few more coins, that'd pay for the stall for another couple of days. He went over to the tack rails, collected his gear, and took it over to Black's stall. The stallion greeted him with a low snort, pawing at the ground, and nibbling softly at his knuckles as he lifted the latch on the half door.

'Yeah, I know you're happy to see me feller, me too. What say we go stretch our legs, shall we, boy?'

Chase gave the gleaming black hide a quick rub down with a twist of straw, and tossed the saddle blanket over the Morgan's broad back. As he did so, something registered somewhere back in his brain, something small, quite insignificant, but not quite as right as it should be.

He stood for a moment, trying to fix whatever it was in his head. Then, just as he'd pretty much dismissed it, and picked up the heavy saddle to place it over the blanket, he stopped, frowned and shook his head. Something really wasn't right.

Quickly, he replaced the saddle over the top of the gate. He pulled the blanket gently off the horse's back, and checked it out carefully. There, right in the centre, very carefully threaded into the coarse weave, so that it would be easily missed until it was far too late, was a long, cruel, needle-sharp, cactus thorn. One that would have done some real damage once the weight of the saddle, and the man, were seated on top of it.

Any horse with a thorn like that sticking into his flesh would be sure to act like a wild mustang. That would be true even of Black, well-trained as he was; the pain inflicted would have been pretty serious, and could easily have caused some lasting damage to the animal. The creature's desperate efforts to flee from the pain could have killed it, or its rider, or both. Chase swore under his breath and looked around the busy stable. Whom should he blame? Who was so very damned determined to get rid of him, one way or another?

Obviously, it was the same *hombre* who'd already tried for him unsuccessfully, twice. But why sink so low as to target his horse? That was some nasty trick. The bastard had already killed an innocent man. Was there nothing he wouldn't do to get rid of his target?

Chase was furious, but knew he needed to remain calm; anger messed with the brain, and addled your thoughts, till you couldn't tell friend from foe. That wouldn't do. That would get a guy killed fast. Whatever happened here, he needed to keep a straight head.

Carefully now, he checked over every inch of the heavy blanket, then he checked and double checked all the rest of the tack, paying particular attention to the girth; that was, as he knew only too well, a favourite place for sabotage. Cuts made part-way through the leather ones, almost invisible to a casual glance, would cause the strap to break when the rider was at full gallop, with deadly consequences. Thorns and burrs inserted in the woven ones caused pain and panic in the mount, who would try every trick it knew to unseat the rider and escape from the pain.

There were many ways to cause injury, or even death, to the horse, or rider, or both, by messing with part of the tack in some subtle way. Now Chase carefully checked over every other piece of his gear, inch by inch, before placing any of it on the horse, and just for good measure, he ran his hands all over Black's body and legs again, although the animal was behaving in his normal quiet way.

There was no real need to believe the stallion had been

hurt, or interfered with in any way, but it didn't do any harm to check him out, given the circumstances. Someone really didn't want Chase here and, as yet, he was no nearer to finding out who it was. He might as well have been chasing a ghost. Satisfied that the gear was all fine, he tacked up Black, noticing that some of the other riders were looking at him curiously as he continued his checking, but he ignored them, and, when all was done, led Black outside.

Chase mounted up and, with a brief but searching look around the area, he headed Black in the direction of the Bar H ranch. The stallion pranced and skittered at first, glad to be out of the confines of the stable and on the road again; restless, like his owner. Chase smiled and let him have his head for a while, before bringing him back down to a measured trot.

The dirt road out of Poynter led north, heading out towards the next town on the trail, Jonesville, which was a long day's ride away. Along the dusty trail were scattered the gateways and signs of various homesteads and ranches. Some were old and past repair now, others looked like they'd been repaired in recent times.

Chase knew most of them; he'd grown up here and most of the names were familiar. Maybe they were owned by different people now but, on the whole, they'd kept the old names. Some though, had vanished completely now. Smaller places, most often bought out by their more affluent neighbours, the land simply swallowed up into their grazing.

He noticed, with an unexpected pang of sorrow, that the sign for the Lazy M had finally gone. The remains of the old gateposts that had once marked the start of the path down to the ranch were broken, and all but invisible beneath weeds and dirt, their stumps standing like gravestones, ragged symbols of the tragedy that had occurred there all those years ago.

The last of the land that had made up the M had been partly bought out, not long after the fire, by old Job Harrison; who owned the Flying Q, to the south of the spread, and some by Jake Parker of the Bar Double P to the north, Annelise had told him.

The M could have been owned by Chase now, if only things had been different. But that had been years ago. Far too many years ago. But somewhere within the core of him there was still that sharp, stabbing pain of a most deep and heartfelt loss.

He shook his head to clear it, and urged Black on into a faster pace.

'No use in cryin' over spilt milk, eh lad?'

He urged the horse onward, at a steady, loping trot. Further along the trail he saw the new sign to the small spread that was the Bar H, and headed on through the gate, looking around him at the land, and the few animals on it. It was sparse grazing, but then it was all sparse around this way, and the few cattle that were making the most of it looked to be in reasonable condition, considering.

He could see the house as he turned into the gateway; this wasn't really much more than a small homestead, not a full working ranch. There was a small clapboard house with a barn close by, and an old buggy, which, although usable, had certainly seen much better days, was standing out front in the yard.

The yard itself was in need of a real good clean-up; pieces of equipment, too old, or too broken, to be of any real use, lay around the edges, and were being gradually overgrown by the sparse scrub and sagebrush that was scattered all around the place.

A ragged flock of chickens picked around the buildings,

looking for anything that might be edible. Tumbleweed had gotten caught in some of the corners, scraps of broken wood and twisted metal lay in haphazard heaps against the barn walls. The roof of the barn was riddled with holes, some of which had been patched with scraps of mismatched wood and sheets of metal. Its battered door hung askew on one big, rusty hinge, jammed half-open.

The house was in sore need of a good lick of paint, to say the very least. The rail around the veranda was broken in places, although he did notice that the curtains at the small windows looked clean and fresh. A string of washing was making no effort to dry itself in the heat, and there was a small wired-off enclosure with a few herbs and vegetables trying to make it through the parched ground. The whole darned place was in real sore need of a man's hand.

A couple of horses, an old flea-bitten grey, and a chestnut, were standing quietly, heads down, tails flicking lazily at the flies, resting, in a small corral close to the house. As Chase approached one of the horses looked up and whickered a soft greeting. Black tossed his head, he wouldn't make any sound. The horses returned to their rest, momentary interest gone.

Suddenly, a whirling red dervish flew from nowhere, in a cloud of dust, straight for them. Black pranced backwards to keep out of its reach. Chase instinctively went for his gun, then, almost as quickly, he realized the situation, and dropped his hand with a smile.

A huge, long-legged red hound strained at the end of a thick chain, attached to an old kennel at the side of the veranda. The kennel was vibrating with every lunge the beast made, and looked as if it couldn't stay standing much longer if it got too much more of that sort of treatment. The hound's jaws were snapping together loudly, froth flying from its maw as it strained out to reach them. Its wild eyes followed them closely, and it carried on barking as they went on towards the house. Black was ignoring the hound completely, realizing that no danger was coming from that quarter now.

As they approached close to the old buggy, a window in the side of the house flew open, and the muzzle of a rifle poked out. A woman's voice cried out loudly.

'Hold it right there, mister!'

Chase raised his hands to show her that he wasn't armed, and Black carried on walking slowly forwards.

'Take it easy, ma'am, I don't mean you any harm, I'm just here to—'

A shot from the rifle landed close to Black's feet, sending up a fountain of dust. Black flinched, his muscles twitched, but he kept on slowly moving forward. The big dog ran off and cowered in its rickety kennel. Chase squeezed his legs on the horse's sides, and Black stood dead still.

'I said, stop – right there, mister! What is it you want?'

'It's OK, we've stopped. I'm not going to hurt you, ma'am. I just wanted to ask you about a kid called Petey. He lives here, right?'

'Petey? Why? What's happened? Where is he? Is he OK?'

The questions were fired off in quick bursts at him, more like challenges than questions, but it proved that she at least knew the boy.

'So you do know him, ma'am. Relax, he's fine, as far as I know. I just wanted to ask you about him. Is he here right now?'

'*No*, I don't know where he is. Why do you want to know about him, mister? Is he hurt?'

'No, ma'am, not as I know of anyways. Just checkin' he's OK is all. He's not been around the livery for a day or two. I kinda like the kid. Just seein' if he was all right, is all.'

'Take off your hat mister; let me see your face.'

Her voice was edgy, nervous. He could see the front of the rifle shaking. Chase tipped the Stetson back so the sun could light up his face, and he looked directly and unblinkingly at the window. There was a long pause.

'Petey's just fine, mister. He was here last night. Thanks for askin'.'

'Ma'am, would you mind lowering the gun please? It's kinda hard to talk with that thing pointed at my head.'

'Then I suggest that you leave, mister, and you don't come back any time soon.'

'The name's Chase, ma'am, Chase Tyler; my sister's called Annelise Murdoch. You might be acquainted with her, she runs the general store over in Poynter, with her husband, Bill.'

He was aware of a longer than normal silence whilst she took in what he'd said. He couldn't really see her through the window; the shadows from the overhanging roof were too dark across the glass, but he knew she was processing that last piece of information. At last with a jerk of the rifle, she called out, with what seemed to Chase to be an even more angry tone in her voice.

'Look, I don't really give a damn who in the hell you are, mister. Just you get off my land, right now. Savvy?'

The gun moved again in the window, and Chase knew that she was drawing a bead right on him, and that this time she meant it. He also knew, instinctively, that this woman could really shoot. Most women just made a show of holding a gun, and their threats were usually empty, but this one, she meant real business. He figured she'd had to learn to use a firearm for real plenty of times before now.

'OK, sure, we're leaving right now, just goin' to turn

round here, ma'am, if that's OK by you, and then we'll be on our way.'

He kept his hands held high where she could see them as he turned Black, using his legs, and they headed slowly towards the gate. Chase turned his head to look over his shoulder. The gun was still pointed at him; he called back,

'Ma'am, there's really no need for you to be afraid of me, just ask around town, and if you do need any work doin' out here, well, I guess I'll be stickin' around hereabouts for a while.'

He'd taken in the fact that the place was in sore need of more than a little care and attention; a woman and a kid like Petey, no matter how strong he might be, couldn't possibly do some of the many things that he'd seen needed doing here. Not by themselves.

'And how do you suggest I pay you for this work, mister?'

Her voice was softer now, almost as if the idea had already occurred to her.

'A home-cooked meal, and a coupla pots of strong coffee'd buy a good couple of hours' of my time, I guess, ma'am.'

He smiled back at the window, nodded, replaced his hat, touched his fingers to the brim in salute, and urged Black away from the house. Her voice followed him as the huge red dog strained to reach them.

'I'll bear that in mind, stranger. But I don't need no one's help; me and my little brother, we do all right on our own, so just you keep away. If'n I see you round here again there won't be no warnin' next time, and then . . . then . . . I won't be aiming at the dirt.'

He silently waved a hand in acknowledgement, and urged Black into a measured trot out on to the Poynter road.

'Well, old feller, 'Lise was right; she sure is one hell of a wildcat, ain't she?'

Black snorted loudly and nodded his head emphatically; Chase laughed and stroked the thick, long mane absently.

'She kinda reminds me of. . . .'

He shrugged, shaking the spectres of the old memories to the back of his mind again, drew himself up in the saddle, eased back into it, and headed back towards town.

His room at the Dime was a small one, but it was pretty comfortable, and Chase reckoned he'd maybe stick around town for a while. Someone was sure as hell out to get him; he needed to know who and, even more, why they were so damn keen to see him dead.

Rather than scare him off, like they might have done with a lesser man, the recent attempts on his life had just served to make him more curious, not afraid. His plan had originally been to visit with his sister for just a short while, two or three days perhaps, and then take off again like he usually did. But now, he was curious. He really needed to get to the bottom of this.

It certainly wasn't any ghost that had it in for him; he had a real live flesh-and-blood adversary. But why? And who?

If someone did want him dead, then was his sister in danger too? And what about her kids? He couldn't let anything happen to them, they were his world.

He needed to find himself some work if he was going to stick around, so the following day he asked around town, and was given a few odd jobs about the place, just about enough to pay his board and lodgings, and for the livery for the next few days.

He'd be staying until he'd laid this particular ghost, that was for sure.

CHAPTER SEVEN

Chase's first few days around Poynter were uneventful.

He'd seen Bill around town a few times, Annelise had invited her brother over to have his meals with them almost every day; sometimes he went, but mostly he took his meals at the small eatery attached to the hotel.

Petey had been back once or twice since that first evening, much to Chase's relief. At least the boy was OK, and he sure was a good little worker. He was really taken with Black, and spent a long time grooming, and talking to him. The horse seemed to have taken to Petey in turn, and stood as quiet as a mouse all the while the boy was working in his stall.

Chase was being extra vigilant whenever he tacked up Black, and wouldn't even trust Petey with that task. He'd got himself some fencing work out at the Parker ranch, the Bar Double P, a couple of miles out of town. Fencing wasn't his favourite job by any means, but it paid, and he'd take whatever might be offered.

Having searched the sky for weather signs that morning, and figuring it would be a good enough day to finish off the job he had in hand, Chase left the hotel early and headed out for the livery. He saddled up carefully, sharp eyes scanning the tack for trouble as he did so, and eventually headed out to the Parker place.

The day was hot, dry, and wind free, it wasn't too long before he had shrugged off his jacket and vest in an all too vain effort to cool down some. Manhandling the fencing posts around, and swinging the heavy pick and hammer were tiring, hot work, and there were no trees way out here to provide even the smallest bit of shade. He stopped, wiped the sweat from his face with his bandanna, and went over to where he'd laid his saddle and pack.

When he'd arrived out at the fence site that morning he'd unsaddled Black, letting him loose to find whatever grazing he could. He'd dug a hole with the fencing shovel, and buried his canteen of water under the saddle, to prevent the heat of the sun making it too warm to be palatable. Chase pulled out the canteen, opened it, and as he took a swig he glanced at the sky. Almost noon he reckoned, pretty soon time to head back to the ranch for the promised meal; it couldn't come soon enough.

He used some of the precious water to wet his bandanna, retied it around his neck, a small frisson of cool wetness making him shiver momentarily, and looked around him. His eyes were drawn then to the near horizon. From the west a plume of grey dust, rising high and moving fast, caught his attention.

Some more hands riding in for their meals? No, Parker had already said he couldn't afford to employ many men, and, aside from Chase, there were only two paid hands. One was out riding herd, and the other was clearing the watering hole.

He knew neither of them was off out in the direction of the dust plume. Besides, from the amount of trail dust that was rising up, there were more than just a mere two riders, and they were approaching the spread pretty fast. Chase shrugged on his vest again, and buckled on his gunbelt. He had a feeling he might just be needing it right about now.

Chase called Black over with a low whistle and saddled him up quickly. Black had seen, or heard, the rapidly approaching riders too, and stood quietly, looking over in their direction, head up, ears moving, nostrils flaring wide to collect the scents.

Four riders drew near, their rangy horses dusty, pushed hard, and so sweated up that the lather flew from their chests as they galloped towards him. Chase could see already that this wasn't a bunch to be trifled with. His senses began to prickle. Here rode real Big Trouble for someone. As the riders drew closer to him he narrowed his eyes and surreptitiously began to take in the details of each man.

One of them was a middle-aged, fat-bellied Mexican, with a thick white scar down the side of his heavily jowled, darkly stubbled neck, and teeth blacker than his scrawny horse's hide. Said horse's hide had been deeply scarred and bloodied by the long, sharp rowels of the heavy silver spurs the Mex was wearing. He had a Winchester in a heavily ornamented holster attached to the side of his saddle, unstrapped and ready for fast use, and he sported two Colts.

There was a young buck of about nineteen or twenty, with long, thin, greasy hair straggling across his scrawny shoulders, beneath a dirty black Stetson. He rode a dusty, fiddle-headed roan that was sucking in wind with a deep, painful, rasping noise.

The boy sported a long, jagged, recently healed bright-red scar down the right side of his face, and a dusty black eye-patch over the right eye. A pair of old revolvers hung low at his hips, a battered Winchester was strapped to his saddle, and a pair of heavy, almost full, bandoleers were slung casually across both shoulders, crossing over at the centre of his chest. His whole demeanour was cocksure, aggressive and brutish; Chase could see right off that this boy thought he was invincible.

There was an old-timer too, who looked like he'd crawled right up out of the grave to be here; his body was positively skeletal. The clothes hung from his frame as if made for a man many sizes larger than he. His leathery skin was a pale shade of grey, his cheeks were deeply sunk, and his eyes were dark hollows. Chase couldn't help an involuntary shudder pass down his spine at the sight of this man.

It looked to Chase as though he could pretty much see the man's bones beneath his almost transparent pale flesh. He had a straggly grey beard, yellowed from too much tobacco, and was dressed all in black, with a high-crowned black beaver hat, and long, dusty, black frock-coat. This all served to heighten the impression of death, but he also sported a pair of well-worn, battered and scarred irons, and carried himself like he knew very well how to use them.

The fourth man was the obvious leader; he rode tall in the saddle of a big excitable Appaloosa, and there was an air of angry authority to his bearing. He rode without a jacket or duster, with a much scuffed and scarred leather waistcoat pulled tightly across his belly.

His shirtsleeves were rolled up to the elbows, revealing a darkly sun-browned set of strong forearm muscles, badly scarred, and with sinews and veins that looked like twisted whipcord. The hair that could be seen beneath his hat was thin, and as white as the mountain snow.

As well as his two handguns, and the rifle at the saddle, he sported two large hunting knives. His wide face was deeply creased, pockmarked, and peppered with scars, and his mouth was formed into a permanent sneer, due to an old, thick scar that sliced through the side of his mouth and down to his chin. The man rode with a hard arrogance that Chase had seen so many times before. The kind of arrogance that he knew always meant trouble for somebody.

As the four riders drew closer Chase tensed and readied himself for whatever trouble might come. He'd been weighing up each member of the group carefully, since they had first come into his field of vision. He swigged at the water casually, wiped his mouth with the back of his hand, corked the canteen, hung it over his saddle horn, and stood easy, waiting for them to pull to a skidding halt beside him. The cloud of dust stirred up by the four riders swirled into the hot dry air, almost choking Chase as they drew closer.

'You Parker?'

The leader spat the words out like venom.

'And if I am?'

Chase replied quietly, carefully taking in all the details he could of the four, without it looking too obvious. They'd been riding for quite a while, the dust lay heavy on their clothes, and their mounts were panting hard. Blood and sweat mixed together into a pink foam on their sides where the rider's spurs had cut in to urge them on. The Mexican grunted and spat a pool of dark brown sputum at Chase's feet.

'That gringo, he ain't Parker, boss, he ain't old enough.'

'Where's Parker at?' the leader asked, looking around the place, eyes lighting on Black, spotting real pay dirt. This was a real fine animal, and he could see it was worth a lot of dollars. His mind was already working out the best way to get it.

'Who is it wants to know, mister?' Chase retorted, sensing trouble; he'd seen exactly where the man's gaze had lighted. To the casual observer Black was standing calmly and quietly, but to Chase's experienced and knowledgeable eyes, the animal was wound up like a watch spring, and ready to move fast. He too, could sense trouble, and like his master, he was more than ready for whatever might come.

The one-eyed boy pushed his horse closer to Chase, until its hot, sweating shoulder was brushing up against him. He kicked out at the older man, catching him on the arm with the heel of his boot. Chase staggered and almost fell, but knew better than to draw his iron too soon.

'That wasn't very polite, was it, son?' he said, quietly through gritted teeth, holding on to his throbbing arm, itching to take the arrogant little bastard down.

'Answer the question then, *old man.*'

The boy sneered, looking around the group for approval, and placed the emphasis hard on the last two words, both of which served to raise Chase's hackles even higher. The others laughed at the comment.

'And if I am Parker, who in the hell are you, and what's your business with me?'

'Nah, you ain't Parker, like he says, you ain't old enough. And if you was Parker, you wouldn't have any need to ask who we are,' sneered the leader, spitting on the ground.

The one-eyed boy shifted in his saddle, one hand moving almost imperceptibly towards his gun. Chase's sharp eyes didn't miss the small movement.

'Let me take him, Pa, you can see he's just playin' us along.'

'Hush up boy. Mister, we don't got no truck with you, just you tell us where old man Parker is and then we'll go and leave you alone, all peaceable like. Won't we, boys?'

He smiled widely and looked around at his men; obediently the others nodded and agreed with broad smiles on their faces, but with that look of a lie deep down in their eyes.

'He's got to be around here somewhere; this here's his spread, we know that for sure. Why're you protecting him, son? He's not your kin, is he?'

The leader looked around, eyes narrowing, scanning the area suspiciously for anyone else.

'Nope, he's not my kin.'

'You just jobbin' for him, then?'

'That's right, and this here's his private land, so I suggest you fellers up and leave it, right about now.'

The four shifted in their saddles, and laughed, and Chase saw the Mexican's hand creeping closer to his gun. Chase's gaze flicked from one to the other; he was getting the full measure of them now. All wind and spit, puffed up like turkey cocks, and not a decent fighter among them, they posed no real threat to him. He'd taken on worse than them in his time, much worse. Still, he prepared himself for the inevitable clash that was to come.

The cadaverous man, who'd remained completely still on his equally bony and still horse, and had stayed silent up till then, watching everything that was going on around him, suddenly spurred his horse round to stand right in front of Chase, looking down at him with a darkly sinister stare.

The others pushed their animals forward until they hemmed Chase in between them.

'You tell us where the old man is, son, and we might just think about lettin' you live.'

His slow, sonorous, voice was as chilling as his countenance. Chase shivered involuntarily, but kept his gaze steadily fixed on the cadaverous man.

'And what happens if'n I don't know where he is?'

The thin man looked off into the far distance, chewing on a wad of dark tobacco, weighing up the words for a long moment, before he spoke again. He spat on the ground in front of Chase. The other three were silent, eyes flitting between Chase and the older man. It appeared as if they were holding their breath, waiting for some gem of great wisdom to drop from the old man's lips. When at last he did speak, his voice was sepulchral. He raised one eyebrow, and shrugged his shoulders nonchalantly, still looking off into the distance.

His answer was chillingly simple.

'Then . . . you die.'

The one-eyed boy laughed out loud, showing a mouth filled with crooked and broken teeth, and started walking his scrawny horse around the outside of the small group. Chase had checked them out well enough now, and knew from long and very painful experience just exactly whom he should target first.

'D'you mind tellin' me, mister, what you want ol' man Parker for anyway?' he asked, with artificial civility, all the while flexing his muscles, and tensing himself for what he knew was coming.

'Mind your own!'

The boy kicked out again. Just as he did so Chase dropped to the ground, reaching up as he went, and quickly grabbing hold of the leader's leg, and not the boy's. Using the element of total surprise he completely unbalanced the man, and pulled him from his shying mount, As the man fell heavily to the ground with a loud grunt of pain, Chase had already drawn his gun and fired up point blank at the Mexican, who hit the floor like a ton of dirt in a cloud of dust, a look of stunned surprise freezing itself on to his ugly fat face.

Black, seeing the trouble begin, took off like a loose cannonball. The leader's horse, unexpectedly freed of its burden, took off after him, reins and stirrups flying, followed closely by the fat Mexican's bony, scarred animal, also suddenly freed of its heavy load.

The cadaverous man, completely shocked into confusion by Chase's sudden action, wheeled his own horse, and instinctively headed to go after Black and the other horses, but then, loyalty won out, and he thought the better of it. Quickly he turned his scrawny horse, and returned to try and rescue his leader, who had pulled one of his knives, and was locked in a fierce hand-to-hand battle with Chase.

The Mexican lay motionless, face up, spread-eagled in the dust, blood seeping from the death wound at his heart, a look of stunned surprise still freezing on his face.

The one-eyed boy had dismounted now. He had pulled a gun and was whimpering and dancing from foot to foot, waving the piece around ineffectually, afraid to shoot for fear of hitting his father, who was rolling around in the dirt with the knife in his hand, while Chase was trying his best to wrest it from him. The blade was heading perilously close to Chase's throat. The two men were ill-matched, the older man was the heavier, but Chase was faster and more supple.

The cadaverous man, more experienced in such things, had no such qualms as the boy, and, quickly and coldly, he fired two successive rounds, bang into the middle of the tussle. Chase, having realized exactly what was about to happen, and with lightning reflexes, quickly managed to turn both himself and his enemy, so that he was almost underneath the white-haired man, who had then raised himself up, knife held high, ready to strike at the man beneath him. Both slugs hit the leader, point-blank in the back.

The white-haired man died almost instantly, a look of shocked surprise on his face as he fell heavily on top of Chase, who quickly heaved him off and threw his body to the ground. As quickly as possible he jumped to his feet. The old man hesitated then, just one awful moment too long, as if he had suddenly just realized the seriousness of what he'd done.

The boy, who was shocked and angered now, turned with a blood curdling scream of rage, and before the older man could raise his gun to fire again, or turn and spur his horse away, the boy immediately shot at him, not at Chase. It was a point-blank heart shot. It could not have been cleaner. As the old man fell stone dead from his mount, Chase was up again, and grabbing for his own piece.

When the boy turned back to try and draw a bead on him, Chase dropped to the ground, rolled forward quickly, and fired upwards, just once. The boy instantly went down like a felled tree, in a cloud of dust, with a strangled, choked-off cry, and a neat round hole in the centre of his forehead welling up with blood, which began to trickle down into his ears, as he lay breathing his last in the dirt.

The other two horses had started off, running now also. Afraid and tired, they didn't get very far before they slowed down, and stopped, standing awkwardly, shifting from foot to foot restlessly, and breathing hard. Chase whistled, and Black trotted back towards him. All the other horses, seeing an animal that was unafraid, followed the natural leader.

Chase looked around him at the carnage. At least he knew they hadn't been whoever had shot at him previously; they weren't by any means clever enough for that sort of working out, and they weren't here to get him. They'd wanted Jake. But still, they'd got a damn sight more than they'd ever bargained for.

'Now then boy, let's get this sorry herd of cayuses over to old man Parker, and fetch a buckboard to pick up the remains.'

He picked up the trailing reins of the four tired animals, swung easily up on to Black, and headed for the ranch house, the scrawny bunch of horse flesh dragging along behind.

He ignored the growing flock of buzzards that were already circling overhead. He knew just what they would be doing almost as soon as he was out of range.

Jake Parker was sitting in his rocker on his veranda, feet up on the rail, smoking, as he watched the approaching dust cloud. A gaunt man, in his late sixties, with thick unkempt pepper and salt coloured hair, he'd expanded his folk's place after they'd died; he'd bought up sections of land around his place as they came up for sale, and now he held quite a portion of the land hereabouts. Indeed it was he who now owned most of what had made up the old Lazy M, where Jess and her family had once lived.

He stood up at the rail in order to see better who was heading his way. He sighed with relief as he watched Chase ride up with the extra four horses, and came out to greet him, a wide smile on his craggy face.

'What's all this, son? Send you out to fix a fence, and you bring me four new horses. My, but they're a sorry-lookin' bunch, though. Where'd you get them from?'

He ran a practised eye over the tired-looking remuda and frowned. Chase dismounted, and threw the four pairs of worn reins over the hitching pole.

'Their riders are feeding the buzzards in the dust, out where I was working. They wanted you, Jake; they asked for you by name. A fat Mexican with a scar down his face, a one-eyed boy, an old feller, looked like a walkin' corpse, and a vicious white-haired son of a bitch, the boy's father. Who in the hell were they, Jake, and why did they want you so bad?'

The old man's smile faded fast as Chase described the

86

gang. He turned away from the other man's sharp, blue gaze.

'The Hastings gang,' he whispered, almost to himself.

'Yeah? So that's the who, Jake, now how's about the why?'

The older man shrugged, and kept his back to Chase as he explained.

'I owed them money; a lot of money. It was a long time back. I moved away, came out here to take over my folk's place. Hell fire, son, I thought they'd forget about me. Looks like they found me at last though, and they were coming to cash in. You took out all four of 'em on your own? Hell, thanks, Tyler, I sure owe you one.'

He turned back to face Chase again, and smiled some-what ruefully.

'I guess that's my debt to them well and truly settled then, huh? I'll get Don to take the buckboard out and get them in to town for burial.'

Chase frowned at that remark; it would mean that the townsfolk would soon get to know that he'd killed all four men. He wouldn't be welcome in the town then, not even if he could prove he'd killed them in self-defence. And he couldn't prove that, not without a witness. Which he didn't have.

Annelise wouldn't be at all happy, and Bill would sure have some ammunition against him then, but there was nothing for it: those four bodies just couldn't be left lying out there on the open range. They had to have some sort of a burial.

Jake Parker saw the look that passed fleetingly across Chase's face and paused. He carefully weighed up the young man who was standing in front of him. From his many years' experience of drifters and wranglers he knew that his next comment was going to sit fairly easy on the younger man's broad shoulders.

'I guess we could just bury them over in the canyon some-where?' said Jake. 'You did me one hell of a favour today, Tyler. I reckon I can do this one for you.'

Chase shrugged, and smiled crookedly and somewhat sheepishly, at the older man.

'It's your land Jake. If'n that's what you want to do, well, I'd sure be grateful.'

He knew Jake had him figured OK, but he also knew Jake owed him, big time now, and he was a man who would pay his dues.

'Sure is my land, and who in the hell is gonna come way out here looking for those sons of dance-hall whores anyway? I'll go get the buckboard son; you ride back out there and clean 'em out. Must be some stuff we can take over into Jonesville, or somewhere, and sell on.'

Chase sighed and nodded; it would be OK.

'Yeah, sure thing. Hey, thanks Jake, I'll meet you out there. Just one thing though, Jake, my name's Chase, not Tyler, that's my last name. I'd be most obliged if you'd use my given name, if you don't mind?'

Jake acknowledged his request with a smile and a hand touched to the brim of his Stetson as he turned to go and fetch the buckboard. Chase quickly stripped the four tired animals of their worn and tattered tack, throwing it all over one of the rails, and deposited the scrawny animals safely in the corral, before remounting Black and riding out once more.

The buzzards were pretty busy when he got back to the scene of the fight. Piled on top of each of the four corpses, two or three deep, and fighting crazily for the tastiest morsels, their large vicious beaks were dripping red. Blood was drying in pools around the bodies. Rags of torn, raw, flesh were lying on the ground.

Chase scared them off with a shot over their heads. They flew up noisily, looking like a ragged black cloak in the wind. It was a sight he'd gotten used to over the years, men who had become buzzard-bait but, all the same, it was one he still didn't much like seeing this close up.

Reining Black in, Chase looked around to make sure there was no one else about. Eventually satisfied that he was alone he dismounted and began the bloody and dirty job of searching the torn and stiffening corpses, ignoring those buzzards that were still hanging around to clear up.

He was kneeling beside the Mexican, unbuckling the silver rowels, when he heard the buckboard coming. He stood up. Jake drew up alongside the men, and looked around; he shook his head and whistled slowly.

'Chase, you're one hell of a guy to have around, takin' out all four at once!'

'No Jake, not me, I only did three, the old guy over there was shot by that one.'

He indicated the thin man, and bent to take the gun belt from the fat Mexican, whilst at the same time trying not to look at the now torn and ragged flesh that had once been his face.

Jake laughed out loud.

'Hell, Chase, three of the Hastings gang is enough at a go! Why not stick around for a while, lad? I could sure use you for a lot more than just fence fixin'.'

Chase wasn't about to ask what else Jake could use him for, and carried on with his gruesome work. Jake got down from the buckboard to help with the task.

When they'd taken everything that could be sold from the bodies they slung the corpses into the back of the wagon, covered them up, and with Jake leading the way, and Chase following closely on Black, they headed out to a distant area of dry canyon, on the furthest southern corner of Jakes' large spread.

There they wasted no time in digging a wide, deep hole. Then, together, they threw the four men into it, without hesitation or qualm. Covering the bloody bodies with dirt, and then heavy boulders, to prevent marauding coyotes and buzzards from dragging out the remains, the two men worked in silence, each one lost in his own thoughts.

No words of prayer were said over the makeshift grave, none was needed. As they headed back to the ranch house the silence continued, until at last Jake broke it.

'Y'know, Chase, I ain't about to ask you where you learned to fight like that, nor what sort of business you might have been in. I don't want to know any of that, but there's a job here for you, permanent, if'n you want it. I need a good foreman to keep the place rollin' along for me.'

'Nope. Thanks, Jake, but I'm gonna be heading out again soon, If'n I live that long, somebody's already tried to kill me a coupla times since I got here this time.'

'Any ideas who?'

'Nope. None, only thing I know for certain, it wasn't that lot. I don't come back here often enough, or stay here long enough, to make that kinda enemy here. 'Cept perhaps my brother-in-law, and he'd have to be some sort of a crazy sonofabitch to do something as stupid as that in his own town.'

'You don't reckon it was these guys after you then?'

'Nope. They had no idea who I was, Jake; just wanted to catch up with you is all.'

'Well, look, why don't you bunk down here anyway 'til you're ready to leave? The bunkhouse is set up for a dozen men, and I've only got the two right now, so there's more'n enough room. Be safer for you here than it will in town from what you're sayin'.'

'Well, that's real good of you, Jake; thanks. You know, I might just do that.'

Chase rode back in to town that evening, and went over to the store; Bill and Annelise were both in there, filling up the stock. When he walked in, Bill made a very obvious point of completely ignoring him.

' 'Lise, just come to tell you I'll be bunking out of town from now on, so don't worry if you don't see me around for a while.'

His sister was anxious, and she was curious, but Chase wasn't about to tell her where he was going to be. If his hunch about Bill was right, then the less he knew about Chase's comings and goings the better. Chase was becoming more and more certain that for some reason, Bill was the one behind the shootings; he wouldn't be pulling the trigger himself, of course, but he'd sure as hell have set them up.

But exactly why? Well, that was going to be a tad more difficult to find out.

CHAPTER EIGHT

Chase was visiting with his sister a couple of days after the incident with the Hastings gang. He still hadn't told her where he was staying, and they were sitting at the kitchen table, watching the children play. Annelise had brewed a pot of coffee, and they were discussing ordinary, day-to-day doings, when she startled him by saying,

'How's the accommodation at old man Parker's suiting you then, Chase?'

'How in the hell d'you know I'm bunkin' there? I haven't told you where I'm lodging!'

The look of surprise on her face told him that she'd no idea how she knew.

'I guess Bill must have told me?'

She shook her head and frowned. She didn't sound too sure of the fact.

'No, I haven't told him either, why on earth would I tell him, Sis? He's the last person I'd tell, you know that. I haven't told anybody. Who in the hell knows where I'm stayin'?'

Immediately, he called to mind the other two men he was sharing the bunkhouse with. Bart and Don had both seemed OK. Neither of them made his senses prickle. Both were just temporary, hired hands. Jake only hired when he really needed to, and most often it was just drifters passing through.

Bart and Don had already been there for a while when Chase turned up. He'd told them hardly anything about himself, and he knew, of course, that Jake would have said nothing; he knew next to nothing anyway. One of them must have let slip where he was staying. Probably after they'd had a few drinks at one of the bars. Liquor was sure to loosen any tongue if enough was imbibed.

He'd need to be even more on his guard from now on.

Something that had been bugging him suddenly surged into his mind; he just had to ask.

'Sis, I know you say the store's doing well, but it seems to me as if it's doing a damn sight better than it should be. D'you know where the money's coming from?'

'Chase! What a thing to say! Why, from the stock we sell, of course. Where else would it be coming from?'

'Who does the bookkeeping for the business, 'Lise?'

'Why, Bill of course. I wouldn't have the first idea about that side of things. I just sell the goods in the shop whenever I'm needed.'

He looked around the place. There had been a heck of a lot of work done to the whole place since he'd been here last. Surely a small general store couldn't earn enough to pay for all those changes?

'Bill's away quite a lot, "delivering goods", isn't he 'Lise?'

'Yeah, but if people want their goods delivered, we'll do it; it helps them out, and that's always a good thing. Folks are always real busy these days, aren't they? If we can help by delivering their provisions out to them, then surely that has to be a bonus?'

'But he's often away overnight too, isn't he?'

Chase had been keeping a close eye on Bill's movements lately. There appeared to be no need for his brother-in-law to stay overnight at any of the outlying spreads. Even with the buckboard, he should have been able to make it home in time to sleep the night in his own bed. His sister frowned.

'Yeees. If he's out that far, he'll go on into Jonesville and stay the night, and he'll pick up any more provisions we might need at the same time. He sometimes has a game of cards with friends. But. . . ?'

She couldn't understand where his line of questioning was going.

'I reckon he's been up to no good, Sis, but I can't figure how yet,' Chase murmured, almost to himself. His sister stood up abruptly and stamped her foot hard, anger flashing from her steely blue eyes.

'Chase Tyler! You've hated my husband since you first set eyes on him, and now you're trying to blame him for some sort of wrongdoing, without any reason! I reckon you'd better leave my home, mister. Right now!'

Chase was shocked at her outburst.

'But Sis, you must know that a little store like this can't keep on growing and prospering, not here. He's getting the money from some place else. He's got shares in the Three Dice saloon you know? And in the gunsmith's. And he keeps a strongbox at the bank.'

Chase had been doing some digging for himself; his brother-in-law had his fingers in a fair few pies around the town. Annelise sat down hard, eyes still flashing in anger, fists tight clenched on the table, exhaling heavily in exasperation.

'I know you hate him, Chase, but what in the hell is the matter with you? Why are you checking up on him? What right have you got?'

'Because I know he's up to no good, but I just don't know what the hell it is yet.'

'That's just plain stupid. You can't just accuse him of something without even knowing what it is. Oh Chase, it's not right. He's a good man, he is, truly.'

'I ain't accusing him of anythin' yet, Sis. Don't tell me you really haven't wondered where the money comes from, though?'

Her silence told him that she might have done, but she was fiercely loyal to her husband, and would never even think to question him.

'Did you know about his shares, Sis? Or about the strong-box? What about that?'

She shook her head for a no, and looked at the floor.

'Sis, I'm going to do a damn sight more checking up on Bill Murdoch, and I'm sorry if'n you don't like it, but somethin's buggin' me about him, and I can't get a handle on it just yet. I will though. Believe me.'

He upped and left quickly then, knowing full well he'd upset his sister far more than he'd ever wanted to.

Chase rode into town from Jakes's place later that week to pick up some more provisions from the Murdoch's store. Whilst he was there he spotted a buckboard he thought he recognized. Pulling it out of his memory, he realized that it was the same one he'd seen out at the Bar H. That meant Petey and his sister were in town somewhere. He'd look out for them, and pay his respects; see if she'd decided if she needed any help around the place after all.

He'd been to the store and picked up the things he'd needed, hanging around for long enough to pass the time of day with his sister, and to realize that she wasn't holding any sort of a grudge against him for the things he'd said previously.

He was about to head back to the Double P, when he spotted Petey, walking along the street. There was a woman beside him who, Chase reckoned, must be his sister. They were too far away for him to make her out in detail, so he sauntered on over in their direction.

'Howdy Petey. You OK, son?' Chase asked when he drew close enough.

'Howdy, Chase, yeah, we're fine, thanks for askin'. Sarah, this is Mr Tyler – Chase. I told you about his hoss, the one that understands man talk, remember?'

'Yes I do. Thank you, Mr Tyler, for letting Petey help you out.'

She reached out her hand to shake his and looked up at him. Chase got a real good look at Petey's sister for the first time, and what he saw clear knocked him sideways.

Beneath the demure blue poke bonnet, a tangle of auburn curls threatened to explode from its confines, and the tip-tilted nose was painted with a generous scattering of pale freckles. Her lips were soft and ripe for the kissing. Her smile was as bright as a new dawn. Brighter. And her wide, shining, eyes danced with an emerald fire that made his head swim.

The breath was knocked clean out of his lungs. He felt like he supposed a drowning man must feel. His head was reeling. There, right there, in front of him, as large as life, and twice as pretty, was Jess! His knees went weak. How could it be? She'd died in the fire. They all had. It couldn't be her.

'Jess?' he whispered.

Her name was forced from him, in the very instant that the emerald fire from her eyes reached its home in his lonely heart. The word was but a simple breath leaving his body, yet somehow or other, it had reached her ears, and she looked scared. Her eyes widened in alarm. She looked like she was ready to run from him.

'Mr Tyler, you are quite mistaken, I'm afraid. My name is Sarah, Mrs Sarah Jameson.'

She spoke quietly, still with her hand outstretched, emphasizing the 'Mrs'.

Chase took her small hand in his, and held on to it like a drowning man to a life preserver. Her hand was smooth and soft and warm. His hand was shaking. She was alive. Jess was alive! It could only be Jess.

Chase stuttered. Never usually one to be wordless with any girl in his later years, this one had left him both wordless and breathless. How could she look so like his Jess? Was she a ghost? Had Jess escaped from the fire somehow? If so, where had she been hiding herself all these years? And why?

'Forgive me, ma'am, for bein' so rude. You just look very like someone I-I er – I used to know. A long time ago. She was called Jess, Jess McCloud.'

His eager gaze searched her face for some flicker of acknowledgement. He found none. He felt hollow.

Her eyes darkened, and to Chase's glance it seemed as though they had filled with tears and were threatening to overflow. She shook her head, and lowered it, so he could no longer see her eyes beneath the rim of the bonnet.

'I'm sorry, Mr Tyler, no. My name is Sarah Jameson, not Jess McCloud, and this is my little brother, Petey, but you know him already, don't you?'

Chase nodded silently; he was still holding on to her small, warm hand, and gazing at her like a moonstruck calf. She extricated her hand from his with some difficulty, and quickly turned to leave. Chase needed to see her again. There were a myriad questions racing through his fevered mind. It was Jess, of that he was certain.

There had never been another woman who had made him feel this way. And there had been many women over the years, none of whom had lasted more than a month or two. None had been able to erase the still raw feeling of the pain that burned deep in his heart, and smouldered in his soul. None had been enough to make him want to put down roots. None could fill the space in his heart reserved for Jess.

Somehow, the spectre he still carried deep in his heart wouldn't allow it. Now, here, back in his home town, of all places, he'd found her again. His beloved Jess was alive and breathing. Here. In the very town where he'd lost her, all those years back.

Chase's mind knew for sure that it couldn't be true. There was just no way. Hadn't this girl said she was called Sarah? And then, as his mind began to clear somewhat, he realized that her hair wasn't bright red as Jess's had been: it was a darker shade of auburn; her eyes weren't as bright as Jess's had been.

His head said it wasn't Jess; it couldn't possibly be Jess. There was no way on this good, wide earth that it could be her. His heart pounded, his soul shouted out to Jess.

He drew a deep and trembling breath.

'Ma'am, d'you remember? I came out to your place the other week, looking for some work? You pointed a rifle at me back then. *Do* you have any work needs doin'?'

'Oh yes, I remember. No, we can manage quite well on our own, thank you anyway. Come on, Petey.'

She took the boy by the hand, with an attitude that meant she was going to stand no argument from him. Chase had some reason to believe she didn't have enough money to be able to pay for a hand to come and work for her. He stepped closer to her, and lowered his voice; she was a proud woman, he could tell, and wouldn't want everyone knowing she couldn't afford hired help.

'I'm not asking for any pay from you, ma'am. I'll do the work for free. I kinda like young Petey here. I reckon I could show him how to do some of them jobs that maybe he hasn't been able to tackle up to now. That way, he'll be able to be a better help to you as he gets older.'

He ruffled the boy's hair, just as he would have done to Charlie's. Petey's bright eyes spoke volumes. His sister hesitated for just a moment too long. Petey pulled at her hand and nodded eagerly.

'Sis, I do need to find out how to use some of those tools, and how to do some of the mendin' of the machinery, then I can be an even bigger help to you. If'n Mr Ty— Chase is willin' to help us out, maybe that's a good idea, Sis, don't you think?'

His bright expression melted her resolve. But still she didn't look squarely up at Chase. Her voice was quiet, yet there was a strength there which he was sure he recognized.

'Fair enough then. For a meal, and as much coffee as you can drink. If you would like to come over on Friday morning, Mr Tyler, I've got an old chain harrow that's in real dire need of a service for a start.'

She turned abruptly, without even looking at him again, and headed for the buckboard. Petey smiled broadly up at Chase.

'Be seein' you Friday, then, Chase.'

Petey smiled, jumped in the air, and ran quickly off after his sister. Chase watched them go, his heart still beating fast. He watched her clamber easily aboard the wagon; her sky-blue skirts swaying across her softly rounded hips, a shapely ankle peeking out from beneath chastely raised white broderie petticoats.

Petey jumped eagerly into the back, and waved cheerily at

Chase. Chase waved limply back, and watched until the wagon was out of sight of any man's eyes. He was watching Jess McCloud driving away from him, and he knew it.

With a last wistful glance at the disappearing wagon, Chase went back into the Murdoch store, feeling all fired up, his heart beating like a kid's at his first dance.

Annelise was serving an elderly woman when Chase entered the store. Annelise looked up, saw that it was just her brother, and returned to her customer. Then she glanced up again; she'd seen the look on his face, and something she'd seen in it troubled her for some reason.

She nodded her head towards the back room, indicating that he should go in. He obeyed silently, and sat at the pine table in the kitchen, quietly watching the children playing and laughing in the yard. Moments later his sister came in, rushing straight towards him; something she'd seen in his face had worried her.

'What on earth is the matter, Chase? You look like you've seen a ghost, or worse!'

She sat beside him and placed a warm, soft hand over his own, she was concerned for her brother. She hadn't ever seen him as agitated as this.

'I guess I have, Sis. Yeah, I have,' he mumbled.

His mind was whirling, his heart doing somersaults.

'Why, what is it? You look terrible. Please tell me, Chase. What is it? Has somebody tried to kill you again? Is there anything I can do?'

She got up and crossed over to the stove, where she poured them both steaming mugs of coffee. She gave Chase his, and stood beside him, with hers clutched in both hands.

'No, no one's tried to kill me. Sis, have you talked to that Sarah Jameson much?'

'I have, a few times now; she's quite a nice girl, I think.

100

Keeps herself to herself. Cares a lot for her little brother. Why?'

'Does she remind you of – of – anyone, 'Lise?'

'You know, I did seem to think there was a resemblance to somebody I once knew, but I couldn't rightly place just who that was. Why? Who is she?'

'Jess. It's Jess, Sis, don't you see it? We thought they'd all died, but Jess and her kid brother must have got out somehow.'

His voice was eager, almost desperate. Annelise leaned on the table to support herself, unable to believe what she was hearing. Chase held on to his steaming mug as if it were a life-preserver. His sister was also deep in thought now.

'Now you say it, sure, yes, there is some sort of a resemblance. But Chase, that's all it is. Just an uncanny resemblance. Jess is dead. I'm sorry to be so blunt, but you know she is. She died in the fire. The whole family did. We all know that; we were all there that night. Practically the whole town was. No one could have possibly escaped from that fire.'

Annelise sat down beside him, and placed a hand gently on his arm.

'That girl is called Sarah, and it's just pure uncanny that she looks like she does, and that she has a younger brother. But hell, Chase, there must be hundreds of women with similar looks. And plenty of them with kid brothers. Chase, please, think about this. She's not Jess. You know she can't possibly be.'

'No. No, I know, Sis, I do know. But her eyes, oh God, I know those eyes. She's so like her, Sis, it's just, well – I guess it's just spooked me, that's all.'

Annelise was watching her brother's agitation with concern. She'd seen how Jess's death had torn him apart all those years ago. She'd watched him turn inward, and ride off into nowhere. She'd heard stories down the years, about some of the things he'd done, and she hated them, and wondered: had Jess lived, would he have been a different man?

'I'm going over there tomorrow, Sis, to help her out with an old chain harrow. I'm going to show young Petey how to mend it, and how to use it properly, so he can give her a bit more assistance around the place.'

His face had changed. Annelise could see some of the younger Chase deep in his eyes now, the boy he'd been was close to the surface once more, his eyes were softer, and they seemed more distant.

'Chase, please be careful. She's really not Jess. Can't ever be, you know that. Deep down you do know that. Don't go getting too deep in.'

He stood up abruptly, kissed her tenderly on the forehead, and then turned to leave the store. Looking back over his shoulder, he smiled at her. The brightest, youngest, most carefree smile she'd seen on him in many a year.

'I'm fine, Sis; I'm finer than I've been in a long time. Thanks for the coffee and the pep talk. See you around, hon.'

He turned and headed for the door with a renewed spring in his step. As he reached the door, Bill entered; they collided. Their eyes locked. There was a hardness in Bill's eyes, which was not lost on Chase. He left the store without saying a word to Bill.

As he wandered across to the livery he glanced back at the store.

Bill was standing in the doorway, watching him.

CHAPTER NINE

Chase made it a priority to try and find out more about Bill Murdoch whenever he was in town, and as he began to gather snippets and fragments of tales, and memories from a variety of folk, a picture began to form. A picture of a man who was hard-working, and strangely, to Chase's mind at least, one who was well-liked around the area.

It was easy enough to pull the wool over some people's eyes; only Chase thought Bill seemed to be able to pull it over most people's eyes. He had come to the town following the gold trail. A whole lot of drifters and chancers had descended on the small town around then, and had hung around just long enough to realize that, if there ever had been any gold anywhere near by, it was all panned out by now. Most left after a while, off to some other place to try their luck there; a very few stayed on. Bill was one of them.

He'd caught the eye of Annelise, and pretty soon he'd married her. Way too soon, as far as Chase was concerned. The moment he met the man, he'd felt he was trouble. The thought that this man had married his only sister made Chase's skin crawl, but Annelise seemed happy; and then the kids came along.

In his all too infrequent visits home there had never

seemed a right time to talk to Annelise and ask her just how much she knew about the man she'd married. Chase had found out that Bill had shares in most of the largest businesses in the town, and even some over in Jonesville. He knew there was a private strongbox in Bill's name, as well as a business one, in Poynter's bank, and word was there was one in Jonesville too.

Their store had grown faster than should have been possible, and Bill and the family were never short of anything. Chase had been doing the rounds of the drinking houses on his nights off, and had got to know a few of the local characters quite well. Eventually, he knew, he would learn something more positive, something he could use to face Bill with. And then the fur would well and truly fly.

Friday morning, checking it was OK by Jake, Chase saddled up Black and headed out to the Bar H. He had a chain harrow to repair. And an assistant to train. As he approached the house the big red hound flew from its kennel towards them. Black didn't even flinch this time; he knew there was no real threat from the hound.

'Lie down, Ranger!'

The hound stopped dead at the sound of her voice, and slunk back in to its ramshackle kennel.

'Howdy, ma'am, good t'see you again.' He touched the brim of his hat in salute. 'Where d'you want me to start?'

Chase dismounted at the house and led Black over to the corral. He let him loose with the two animals already there, and threw the tack over the rail.

'The harrow's in the old barn there, Mr Tyler. I'll go find Petey for you.'

She turned back into the cool and shade of the house. Chase heard her calling out to the boy. Some moments later Petey appeared at the door, hurriedly tucking his shirt into his pants, eagerly looking for Chase, and waving when he saw him arriving. He ran over to the barn behind Chase.

'I'll show you where it all is, Chase.'

Over in a dark corner a pile of old machinery stood in a tangle. Chase spotted the harrow, in amongst the stack. It would take some sorting out, even to get the harrow out from under the pile, never mind get it back into working order. He shook his head. There was work enough here to keep him, and Petey, going for quite some time to come.

'OK, Petey, let's get this lot organized first. You get out all the parts that you can manage. I'll grab the bigger pieces and we'll sort them into two piles.'

They both worked hard at sorting all the metal out into its respective parts. By lunchtime, there was a pile of rusting metal that was of no use to any man, and a few pieces of rough old machinery that Chase knew he could get fixed eventually.

'Petey, I've gotta go and get some ironmongery from the blacksmith. You get all those useless pieces over into a pile round back of the barn, out of the way for now, but carefully. I'll be away around an hour or so.'

'Sure thing, Chase, no problem.'

Chase saddled up Black and headed into town. He placed his order for nuts, bolts and other metalwork with the blacksmith, and headed over to see his sister. She was working the shop. Bill was away, yet again.

'D'you know where he is, or what it is he's doin' while he's away, Sis?'

'Don't start again, Chase. He's a good man, and a busy one. He's not one of those felons you're always chasing.'

'Maybe not as far as you know, Sis, but there's somethin' about the guy that just doesn't add up. I think—'

'*No,* Chase! You really *don't* think! That's exactly what's the matter with you!'

His sister's outburst startled him. He took a step backwards, as if she'd smacked him across the face. He frowned down at her.

'Sis?'

'Well hell, Chase! There's nothing wrong with Bill. He might be a bit of a dullard compared to you, and the sort of life that you lead, but that kind of life just doesn't suit everyone. Some people want a peaceful life. There is nothing at all wrong with my husband. Ask anyone; he's a good man. You know what your trouble is, Chase Tyler? Do you? Well, do you?'

She had stepped closer to him as she was speaking, and now stood almost on his feet, glaring up at him, and waving her finger under his nose, for all the world as if he was a naughty child. He shook his head silently for no, still flabbergasted by her anger; she was shaking her fist at him now. He'd hardly ever seen her lose her temper like that. For a moment she reminded him of their ma. He gulped loudly. She carried on with her tirade.

'You don't? Well I'll tell you then, shall I? You're just *jealous*, Chase Tyler. You're jealous of what I've got with Bill. I've got a good husband, a family, money, a nice house. You're just a drifter, a no-good nothing, with nothing!' She pushed him in his shoulder, hard; he took a step backwards, still speechless. 'You've never been able to settle down with anyone, and you're just jealous of me and what I've got! That's what it is, that's what's wrong with you. You're worse than the kids! You'll try anything to discredit my Bill! You've always hated him, because you're jealous of him is all! It's all pure jealousy! Now just you get out of my house! And don't you dare come back until you can say something civil about my husband! *Go! Go now!*'

Chase blinked. He felt as if he'd been punched in the face, hard. The worst of it was that now, in that single moment, like a bolt of lightning, he knew that it was all completely true. Annelise was dead right.

He was stupidly, painfully, jealous of everything she had. Everything he didn't have.

He'd wanted a family, money, kids, a home, once upon a time. But he'd lost all of that a long time back. His best chance of having it had died in the fire, along with Jess.

Seeing his sister with Bill and their kids, well, that had just brought home to him exactly what he had been missing all these years.

Yes, he was jealous; it was the most stupid thing he'd ever heard, but it was dead right.

In all his investigations, he'd heard no bad tales about his brother-in-law, just good. Bill was a good business man. Hard, but fair. And he looked after his family. Maybe Chase did have him wrong. It was an admission which stuck in his craw, but which, he knew now, was probably correct.

' 'Lise, I'm so sorry – I just – I well – I'm sorry.'

He held out his hands in a gesture of defeat; she turned her back on him with a huff. He left the store without another word. He'd never wanted to upset his sister, not in a million years, but that was just what he'd succeeded in doing with his stupidity.

He was smarting from the power of his beloved sister's words, and the terrible mixture of feelings they had aroused in him. Those awful feelings that had been dragged up to the surface by just one word. One very true word.

He was jealous. And he didn't like what it had done to him. He didn't like the feeling.

Jealousy.

CHAPTER TEN

Chase had been working out at the Double P for some time, and had got to know the other two hands pretty well. He was almost certain they were nothing to do with whoever was trying to kill him. He was mostly a good judge of men, and seldom wrong in his judgement. Even though it seemed as if he'd been very wrong about his brother-in-law, he felt he really had no need to worry about the two Double P hands.

Then, as Chase and the other two headed towards the homestead one evening, they saw Jake standing in front of the bunkhouse door with a younger man. Chase's skin prickled as he looked the stranger up and down, and he frowned. Who was the guy, and what was he doing here? More than that, why was his mere presence arousing feelings of impending peril in Chase? The men dismounted, waiting for Jake to tell them what was going on.

'Boys, this here is Mitch, he'll be with us for a while. He was passin' through, and reckoned he'd ask for a spot of work. I guess we can do with an extra pair of hands, eh?'

Chase looked the boy up and down, thinking he looked familiar in some way. Around twenty-four or so of age, he reckoned. Dark hair and eyes, not tall, skinny, he looked like he was in need of a good square meal. His clothes were well-worn and dusty, as if he'd been riding for a long time.

Chase noticed the boy's eyes specifically. Deep-set, with dark shadows, as if from long lack of sleep, and dark brown in colour, so dark that the pupils almost couldn't be seen, making it look as though his eyes were films of deep-brown glass.

The boy returned Chase's stare like for like, unblinking, fixing the older man with that deep-brown gaze. Chase noticed the small movements of the boy's body, movements which told him the boy was drawing himself up to his full height, and puffing out his chest to make himself look bigger than he really was. Sizing up the opposition.

His eyes carried in them a dark fire, a spark of something that made Chase's spine tingle.

'Howdy fellers, Jake here reckons you're a good team, I'm sure looking forward to working with you all.'

He reached out a hand towards them. The other two men didn't hesitate and shook him by the hand warmly, introducing themselves, then turning back to unsaddle and turn out their horses before heading in for their meal.

Chase, however, hesitated just a moment too long; the boy drew his hand back without making contact with Chase in any way, or speaking to him at all, whilst still fixing him with that disconcertingly dark star. Then he turned sharply on his heels and followed the other men over to the corral.

Chase stood and watched him go, a sharp stab of uneasiness twisting in his gut. His senses were tingling. Who was the boy, and what did he want here? His story about passing by just didn't ring true somehow

The boy was a willing worker though, and in the first couple of weeks he turned his hand to almost anything asked of him. And kept his head down. But he avoided contact with Chase whenever they were anywhere close by.

Often though, Chase caught Mitch watching him when he thought Chase wasn't looking. And each time the look in those dark eyes was one of inexplicable hatred.

Old Jake was a creature of habit, and every Wednesday, come what might, he would hitch up the buggy and take his wife off into town for her to do the shopping and meet her friends, while he stocked up on whatever was needed around the homestead, and then joined his cronies for a drink and a couple of hands of cards.

Jake and Chase had come to an arrangement; while Jake was away in town Chase would spend that afternoon at Sarah's place. The other hands were off around the place, doing whatever jobs were on the list for that day. Chase would finish whatever job he'd started that morning, go back to the bunkhouse, have a wash, change his shirt, and head on over to Sarah's for the rest of the day.

He pegged in the last of the wires on the section of fence he was working on, stood up straight, and stretched his back, looking at the horizon. The afternoon was going to be clear; he could get some boarding on the side of her barn today.

Chase rolled up the tools in his pack, saddled up Black, and they set off steadily towards Jakes's spread. Chase would let Black have a quick run there whilst he tidied himself up a bit before going over to Sarah's place.

Back at the ranch house, Chase unsaddled Black, placed the saddle over the top rail of the fence, and let the horse out into the corral, watching as the stallion galloped off, tossing his head, and kicking his heels high, pleased to be free of his gear.

Chase turned and made for the bunkhouse with more than just a hint of a spring in his step, knowing that pretty soon he'd be seeing Sarah again. As he pushed open the bunkhouse door and stepped into the darker confines of the old building, he blinked to adjust his eyes to the lower level of light inside.

Just then, something hard and very heavy hit him on the back of the head with such force, that he was knocked right off his feet and propelled forward hard. He ended up, face down and unconscious, on the bunkhouse floor.

When Chase tried to open his eyes, he groaned out loud, as excruciating pain sliced through his head. He tried to shake it to clear it. That was a bad move, the pain exploded inside his brain, sending red flashes through his head. His eyes felt as if they were glued shut. He tried to reach up to rub at his stinging eyes, but his arms wouldn't obey his thoughts.

Gradually, something approaching full consciousness brought severe pain and the realization that he was sitting in a chair, trussed up hand and foot, with a roll of rag pushed into his mouth for a gag. He'd been in some pretty tight scrapes before, but he had to reckon that this was just about one of the worst.

He tried looking around in the gloom of the low building, but even the slightest movement of his head created intense stabbing pains. He could feel the blood, a warm thick trickle, creeping down his neck and soaking into his shirt. Involuntarily, he let out a groan.

From somewhere behind him then, he heard a low laugh. It echoed sinisterly around the silent building. He struggled, trying unsuccessfully to turn, to look at his captor, and to release his hands from the ropes.

'Hurts, does it, Tyler?'

The voice was that of a fairly young man, Chase guessed, and he thought he recognized it from somewhere, but his head was buzzing furiously, as though a swarm of hornets were nesting inside it, and he couldn't quite make it out.

The guy obviously knew him. Chase struggled again to try and free his hands.

'Don't bother tryin', you're hogtied real tight,' the voice behind him sneered.

Chase stopped struggling then, and took stock of the situation. He was well and truly trussed up. His vision was blurred, and his head felt as if a tomahawk was buried in it.

He couldn't see the guy behind him, but he could hear his breathing, harsh and trembling. He could feel that his assailant was wound up tight as a spring, he was unpredictable, dangerous. But who in the hell was he?

Chase struggled again, and tried to talk through the gag. He tried to push out the gag with his tongue. His mouth was as dry as the desert, the dirty cloth was sucking all the moisture out of it: he wanted to throw up, but he choked it back.

'Mm – mmm – mmm,' he muttered.

The man behind him laughed out loud.

'What was that? I can't hear you, Tyler.'

Chase recognized the voice now that his head was clearing some. It was Mitch. But why? Chase wrenched at his bonds; they gouged deeper into his flesh.

'OK, let's talk then, you goddamn sonofabitch.' Mitch said as he walked round to the front of his trussed-up victim. He pulled up a chair and sat close, staring at him with loathing, an evil smile on his darkly stubbled face. He was tossing a large hunting knife from hand to hand. Chase had no doubt at all that he meant to use it.

'So, Tyler, what was it you were tryin' to say?'

Chase met that hard, cold, stare unflinchingly, even though his head felt as if it was about to burst.

'Mmmm – mmm.'

He tried to swear at the boy, who smiled, or rather, leered in his direction.

'Oh, I'm so sorry. Here, let's fix that, shall we?'

He reached forward, and yanked the rag hard out of his captive's mouth, throwing it to the floor. A bolt of lightning flashed through Chase's brain, and involuntarily he closed his eyes. He tried to straighten his thoughts out. Tried to clear his fuzzy head, to remember what he might have done to this boy. He'd done a hell of a lot of things he wasn't proud of in the past, but he couldn't bring to mind anything which might have involved Mitch in any way.

His arms were going numb now, and his head was splitting. He was in a hell of a difficult situation. The boy wanted to kill him for some reason, and Chase had absolutely no doubt in his mind that, in some way or another, he was going to do just that. Chase momentarily thought of calling up Black, but just as quickly thought better of it; the boy might harm him too.

Unless Chase could extricate himself from the ropes somehow, and soon, he was in real trouble. Each time Mitch turned his back, Chase worked at struggling to free his wrists from the bonds, trying to ignore the pain it was causing, feeling them loosening each time, and ceasing his efforts whenever the boy looked back in his direction.

Opening his eyes again, he looked straight into those of the boy. They were dark, and filled with the fire of a deep-seated hatred. A hatred that left Chase in no doubt at all that Mitch meant every word he spat out. Chase's blood ran cold. He might well not get out of this situation alive.

'Why?' was all he could croak through the bloodied desert that was his mouth.

Mitch leaped up, and smashed his fist hard into Chase's face, whipping the bound man's head back, and causing a bone-jarring pain to shoot through his whole body.

'You want to know why, do you, Tyler?' sneered Mitch as

he sat down in front of Chase again, breathing heavily, and smiling with what looked remarkably like a snarl.

'OK, I guess I can tell you before I kill you. Can't have you meeting your Maker and not knowing why, now can we? Although I don't reckon it'll be your Maker you'll be meetin', Tyler. Rather old Nick hisself, the things you done in your time, eh?'

Chase could feel his bonds slackening now. They'd been tied in haste.

'Do I look in any ways familiar to you, Tyler? I mean from before I came here?'

'Now you mention it, I had been thinkin' I'd seen you some place before. Who in the hell are you, kid?'

'I'm the guy that's already tried to kill you three times before. Sadly, I missed the first time, light was bad up there in the rocks. The second time, well, it was just bloody damn unlucky that the old Chinee got hisself in the way. But how you found that big ol' thorn in the saddle blanket, well I don't know. I thought I'd hidden it well enough. Let's say it'll be fourth time lucky, huh?'

'Why? Why'd you want to kill me, kid? I don't know you. What in the hell have I ever done to you?'

He was racking his aching brain for a reason for Mitch's behaviour towards him, trying to place his face, searching for some incident that they might both have been involved in.

'You want to know what you've done to me, Tyler?'

Mitch was up and pacing now, and his voice was rising with anger. He was hefting his heavy knife back and forth.

'Well, let's start with you killing my ma and pa shall we?'

'No. I didn't—'

He was stopped short by the boy grabbing him up by the shirt front with one hand, holding the point of the knife against his throat with the other, and glaring deep into his eyes.

'No? No? Howdya know you didn't, mister?' Mitch spat. He let go, pushing Chase back into the chair roughly, and continued his pacing.

'Because I ain't never killed no woman, kid. Never have done. I wouldn't do that, it ain't my style, not a woman.'

'Maybe not with a bullet, or a knife, true, but you killed her all right, Tyler. You killed my pa, and then I watched my ma pine and fade away to skin and bone, until she died too. So yeah, you killed 'em both, Tyler. Yes you did, and now you're gonna pay.'

Mitch smashed him across the back of the head with the handle of the knife. Chase's vision turned red, and streaks of lightning flashed around his brain. He didn't cry out though: Mitch would have loved that, and Chase wouldn't give him the satisfaction.

'Who was your pa, Mitch? When did I kill him? Where was it? Why?'

Mitch back-handed him across the face hard. Chase saw stars.

'You just bloody well shut up, Tyler. Too many questions. Too many damn questions. OK. Tuscon. Ten years back. Think, Tyler. Cast your sad old mind back ten years. Oh, I was just a kid then, Tyler; you wouldn't remember my face. You came into town, you joined a big poker game that night. Remember?'

He back-handed Chase across the face real hard, Chase tasted the blood, hot and tinny in his mouth. One eye wouldn't open now, it was so swollen and caked with blood.

'No, I bet you don't; one card game in one town is pretty much the same as any other to you, and one dead man in the dust is just like all the others you killed. Ain't that right?

You accused my pa of cheatin' that day. He called you out, and you killed him, Tyler, you left him crawling like a dog in the dirt, bleeding to death. Then you just up and walked away. He died in the dirt, in my poor ma's arms. Now you're gonna die, Tyler. Slow and painful, for my ma.'

The boy was agitated now, winding up for the kill. Dangerous. Chase could feel the energy sparking off him as he paced back and forth.

'I was just ten years old, Tyler. I had to watch my ma fadin' away. I couldn't help her, nobody could. I tried so hard. I nursed her until I watched her die from her grief. And it's – all – your – fault!'

The last words were punctuated by thumps of his clenched fist into Chase's body. Chase's hands were beginning to work loose from his bonds as Mitch continued to rant and rave.

The boy was explaining, in strongly graphic details, just exactly what he was going to do to Chase to kill him, and then what he was going to do to his lifeless body. He'd had ten years to plot this precisely, and he was going to thoroughly enjoy every second of his victim's torture.

Mitch kept coming back over to hit Chase at regular intervals, and he never let go of the knife. His knuckles whitened with the force of his grip.

Chase was weakening now, his head hanging, bloodied. He really didn't know how long he'd be able to hold out. Curling tendrils of black hair curtained his face, blood was running from his nose, his lips, and the cuts on his face; his whole body throbbed and stabbed with pain, but, at long last, he managed to loose his hands from the ropes. He kept them still behind his back though. He was waiting, gathering what little strength he had left. He was waiting for just the right moment.

116

The boy stopped his shouting and pacing at last, and stood tensely in front of Chase, knife held ready to strike.

'OK, Tyler, so now you know who, and now you know why, so you can die in "peace". Which is a damn sight more than you let my folks do, you bastard.'

As he pulled back his arm to strike with the knife at last, Chase quickly managed to pull his hands free from the rope, dart his aching arms round to the front, and grab the boy's hand, just the merest fraction of a second before the knife reached him. Even in his weakened state, he was still stronger than the boy.

He tightened his grip, twisting and bending the boy's arm back, and feeling it snap like a dry twig in his hands. Mitch screamed out in pain and rage.

Chase let go of the boy's arm with one hand, and caught the knife in one easy movement before it hit the floor. Swiftly, he cut through the ropes which were holding his legs, and whilst the boy was still writhing and holding on to his shattered arm, crying out in agony, Chase landed a hammer blow to the solar plexus of the other man, knocking him right off his feet, and almost halfway across the room.

As quickly as he could Chase stood up and crossed the room, to stand above Mitch, who was crawling on the floor, clutching at his arm, and crying out in agony.

'Sorry I had to do that, kid, but you were going to kill me, or worse, given the chance, so I guess you got off light, eh? OK, so let's start over. Who's gonna do what to who, was it?'

Chase, one eye swollen and closed, his head bloodied and bruised, his wrists dripping blood, bent and took Mitch's gun out of its holster, throwing it across the bunkhouse floor towards the stove at the far end. Mitch was pale, and whimpering now, trying to push himself backwards, scrabbling with his heels across the floor, away from Chase, who was following slowly, knife in hand, towering menacingly above the now desperately sobbing boy.

'Don't kill me. No. Please don't kill me!' he cried.

'No? Why not, kid? You were gonna kill me without no never mind. Why in the hell shouldn't I kill you?'

Chase's eyes narrowed dangerously as he looked down on his tormentor.

'I'm sorry, I'm sorry. Please. No!' Mitch whimpered, as Chase towered over him, imitating the boy's previous hefting of the knife from hand to hand.

'I should just skin you and paunch you out right here, right now, kid. You were only too ready to do it to me back there. Then I guess your hide'd make a good trophy on the barn door, and your head on the gate post.'

'I'm sorry, please, Tyler, no!'

Chase turned on his heels and walked away from Mitch.

'Hell kid, you just ain't worth it.'

'I'm still gonna kill yuh, Tyler!' Mitch spat defiantly, sitting up and holding on to his arm. His fathomless brown eyes flashed dangerously. Chase stopped, but didn't turn round, just glanced back over his shoulder.

'Listen kid, I didn't kill your ma, and I'm truly sorry for your loss. But if your pa was cheatin' at cards, then he got just exactly what was coming to him, and if'n your ma died from pining for him, I'm sorry, but that part really ain't none of my doin'. Now, let me get you over to the doc, and get that there arm fixed. I'm givin' you this one chance to go away and think about things. Make a new life, without all this anger and hatred burning inside of you. It'll eat you up and spit you out. I know.'

'Just leave me be, Tyler. I'll make my own way. But one day I'll get yuh. One day. Or one night. It'll be when you least

118

expect it. When your back's turned. Or when you're asleep. I'll be there, in the shadows, Tylcr. And you'll be dead!'

The venom in the boy's voice chilled Chase to the bone; he knew that Mitch was serious. But he just couldn't bring himself to kill the boy. He might have done a lot of things he wasn't proud of in his life to date, but killing an injured boy in cold blood wasn't going to be one of them.

'Your hoss in the corral, kid?'

The boy murmured a barely audible 'yes', Chase knew the boy's horse, he picked up the discarded gun, tucked it in his belt, went outside, and found Mitch's gear to the side of the bunkhouse. He whistled up Black, who came trotting over to him, with a group of other horses following in his wake. Mitch's was among them. Chase caught and saddled the horse up, and led it over to the bunkhouse, tying it loosely to the hitching rail.

Chase went back into the bunkhouse, grabbed the kid, and yanked him to his feet, Mitch glared at him. The boy's eyes were still defiant even through the pain.

'Do I get my iron back?'

'What? So that you can shoot me in the back right here? I don't think so. I'm gonna give you the chance to think on your life, try and turn yourself around, kid. Letting all this rage and anger churn around inside of you ain't no good for any man. Trust me. You're young enough to make a life that's half-decent, even now. You ride on out of hcre, kid. You don't look back. Don't you even think back, punk. And if'n I see you anywhere here abouts again, it'll be me that does the killin', boy, and you'll be joining your poor ma, and your cheatin' pa.'

He walked behind the boy as he staggered over to the door, still holding on to his arm.

'Right, there's your cayuse, now you just ride out to town,

tell the doc you've had some sort of accident, and when he's fixed you up, you disappear fast. I see you anywheres round here again, it'll be me doin' all those things you mentioned, only then I'll be doin' 'em to you. I'll tell Jake you just lit out after your little "accident".'

Reaching his horse, Mitch stopped and glared back over his shoulder, fixing Chase with his hard, dark, stare.

'Watch your back, Tyler. One day. . . . One night. . . .'

He struggled painfully up on to the back of his horse, and kicked it into a trot. Chase slapped it on the rump to get it moving fast, and watched as the injured boy headed off into the distance. That kid was sure harbouring some real anger, and plenty of grief. Chase would have to keep eyes in his backside from now on. But he'd given the boy a chance, at least, and he hoped that that would be enough to make him see sense.

Chase had himself a good clean-up, dressing his own wounds as best as he could. As he looked in the cracked mirror above the old washstand he almost didn't recognize himself; his eyes were swelling up, one was closed tight, and dried blood was smeared all over his face. His cheek was cut and bleeding, he had a split and swollen lip, there were bruises all over his body, and his head was throbbing like a bass drum, from a lump the size of a large egg on the back of his skull.

His ribs hurt like hell, and he was pretty damned sure some of them must be busted. Riding was going to be pretty difficult in this state. He knew Sarah and Petey would be concerned, but he'd had to patch himself up before now, and stitch up his own gashes too. He'd had worse; he knew he'd survive.

He whistled up Black, who seemed to know there was something wrong, and gently nuzzled at his master's face with his velvety soft, whiskery nose, Chase winced as the horse touched a particularly tender bruise.

'Yeah boy, I'm a bit battered, but I reckon I'll live. Let's go over and see Sarah and Petey, we've got a job to finish. C'mon.'

He saddled up slowly and painfully, and headed off out to Sarah's place, thinking he was going to get on with another of the many jobs over there, thinking about the hate he'd seen in Mitch's eyes. Thinking about Sarah. As they approached the Bar H, Petey ran out to meet them, a bright smile across his face.

'Chase, how're you doi—!' He stopped in his tracks as he saw his friend's face.

'Sis! Sis! Chase is hurt, he's hurt bad! Come quick!' he shouted.

'No, son, leave it. I'll be OK, honest.'

Sarah came running from the house, wiping her hands on her apron. She gasped when she saw the state of his face. Her hands flew to cover her mouth, and she paled visibly.

'I'm that bad, am I?'

He tried to laugh. His ribs stabbed excruciating pain into his side, and his head felt as if it was about to part company from his body.

'Oh, my goodness! What on earth's happened to you?'

She ran to help him. Petey took hold of Black's reins, and Sarah helped Chase down. As he landed on the ground he groaned, and fell to his knees. Sarah dropped to her knees on the ground beside him. She looked up into his beaten, scarred face, and he saw the tears welling up in her beautiful wide green eyes.

'Oh, Mr Tyler, what did they do to you?'

'Hey, I've had . . . ugh . . . worse.' He tried to rise, and gasped as a sharp bolt of pain exploded in his ribs.

'Come into the house, Mr Tyler, let me tend to you. I think you've got some broken ribs; let me bandage them for you.'

'It's all right, ma'am, just a little accident is all, I'm fine. Don't fret yourself, please.'

Petey led Black over to the corral, where he let him loose. Black stayed by the rail, tossing his head and whickering softly.

'It's OK, boy, I'm in real good hands here. Ease up, now.'

The stallion ceased his head tossing, but stayed close by, watching silently, as Petey and Sarah helped Chase into the house. Chase sat shakily at the table. Sarah sent Petey off to fill a bowl with hot water, and fetch some clean rags and a bottle of salve. She poured something from the small brown bottle into the water, and began to bathe his battered face gently.

'You're going to need some stitching. Petey, go get the doc fast, tell him Mr Tyler's hurt real bad, he's needed now. Go. Hurry.'

The boy ran from the house without a word, and harnessed up the old grey as quick as he could. He kicked it into a fast trot and headed towards Poynter.

'Put your hands in the bowl to soak, and I'll clean up your face first. I'll do what I can till the doc gets here.'

When she had finished tending to his face she gently lifted one of his hands, softly cleaning away the blood. The gouges were deep and raw; he winced as she touched them, but didn't pull away the hand she was holding on to so gently. She softly rubbed some salve into the wounds, and wrapped them in clean rags.

'I still need to tend to your ribs. Let me help you get that shirt off.'

'No, ma'am. Thanks, but I'll be fine. I guess the doc'll be

here soon. Petey can kick that old grey mare into a fair gallop when it's needed. He's a good boy.'

'Yes he is; he takes after his father.' She looked at the ground and sighed. Chase knew better than to ask any questions right now.

'Now, are you going to tell me who it was who beat you up, and why?' Her voice had a kind of sternness to it that he heard at times in his sister's voice, and he smiled.

'Nope.' He looked away from her bright enquiring eyes. 'It's done. I'll heal, I've had a hell of a lot worse.'

The doctor's buckboard arrived just then, and Sarah jumped up to go and meet him. The doctor grabbed his bag and followed her and Petey quickly into the house. He whistled long and low when he saw the state of his latest patient.

'Looks to me like you got in the way of a stampede,' he commented, as he opened his bag.

'You should see the other feller,' Chase quipped, trying to smile, and gasped as the pain shot through his ribs again.

'Come on, son, off with this shirt. Let's have a look at the damage.'

Carefully, the doctor helped Chase off with his bloodied, torn shirt. Sarah gasped out loud when she saw the state of his body, and rushed to fill a bowl with fresh hot water for the doctor, who was carefully examining every scratch and bruise. He gently wiped the worst of the blood from some of the cuts, shaking his head and tutting to himself as he did so.

'Hell of a beating you've taken, Mr Tyler. How many were there?'

'Just the one. He jumped me from behind when my guard was down, tied and gagged me, and beat the holy shit out of me. Sorry, ma'am.'

He looked across at Sarah and winced as the doctor prodded at his ribs. Sarah couldn't draw her eyes away from his chest. Broad, strong and tanned, with a covering of dark curls and, right now, dotted with bruises and cuts, and covered in blood. But she was looking beneath the blood, at the broad strong frame of the man sitting before her.

She watched the firm muscles of his arms flexing as he moved, his strong hands, fists clenching in pain at times. Hands which were used to very hard work, but which, she was sure, would be tender and kind. She'd watched the way he treated his horse, and knew he would treat his women just as gently. The doctor spoke then, and startled her back from her dreams.

'Well, ma'am, he's got a coupla broken ribs, possibly some slight concussion, and one hell of a lot of cuts and bruises. One or two I'll have to stitch up. He's strong, though, he'll heal just fine. The ribs'll take a while, but I guess he's had worse in his time.'

He'd seen the old scars which peppered the younger man's body, and so had Sarah. The doctor turned to his patient.

'Not a lot of heavy work for you for a week or two, young man. Coupla days good rest for that cracked head of yours, and you'll be wrangling them cattle again soon enough.'

Chase attempted a laugh, and gasped; it ended up as a loud groan. He smiled weakly up at Sarah as the doctor wrapped a wide bandage around his ribcage and then stitched the deeper gashes on his body and his skull.

'Best not do any hard ridin' for a while, son; in fact, have some bed-rest for a few days until them ribs begin to heal.'

'I'll ask you if I can hitch a ride with you up to Jakes's place, Doc; that's where I'm stayin'. I can lie up in my bunk there for a few days. Jake won't mind.'

The doctor agreed to take him back. Petey went out and tied Black on to the side of the buckboard, then hoisted his heavy saddle into the rear of the wagon.

'Leave your shirt here, Mr Tyler,' said Sarah. 'I'll wash and mend it, and stitch the missing buttons back on. It's the least I can do for the help you've given us here.'

She wrapped a thick blanket around his broad shoulders, and she and the doctor helped him up into the back of the wagon.

'I'm sorry, I guess I won't be around for a while, ma'am.' He smiled weakly.

'That's fine, Mr Tyler. You just rest and get better. You'll be back soon enough.'

The doctor slapped the reins and the wagon headed off, Petey running alongside, waving and shouting to Chase to get better. He ran back to his sister, who stood and watched until all she could see was a cloud of dust on the near horizon.

'Sis, Sis? Did you see all those old scars on his body? Wonder where they all came from? D'you think they was gunfights? Or knife cuts? Mebbe he had some run-ins with some Injuns?' he asked with relish.

'Yes, Petey, I did see, and it's none of our business.'

She turned to go and prepare their meal. She'd seen them alright, all those ragged white scars scattered across that firm, tanned, flesh, and, like Petey, had wondered what they had been caused by. She shook herself back to the task in hand, feeling just a little warmer than the heat from the stove would have normally made her.

The doctor deposited Chase and Black at Jakes's ranch. After telling the old man what was needed, leaving instructions as to Chase's care, he rode off to his next patient. Jake helped Chase into the bunkhouse and settled him down.

'I'll have Ellie fetch you a meal out soon,' said Jake with a frown. 'If this is anything to do with Mitch, you'd best tell me, son. He's gone and lit out, says he had a "bit of an accident", but he went to the doc, and the doc says that Mitch's all cut up too, and he's got a badly broken arm. You two fellers get into a fight?'

'Guess you could say that.' Chase smiled ruefully. 'He won't be back here any time soon, that's for sure, but he's gunnin' for me, Jake. The next time we cross paths one of us ain't gonna make it out. Not unless he starts to see some sense in the meantime.'

Jake shook his head, tutting under his breath, and helped Chase to lie down.

When he woke, Chase's head was still throbbing fit to bust. He moved, and his ribs cracked, he ached in places he didn't even know he had. Trying to sit up, he groaned loudly. Had he been stomped by a herd of cattle ? It sure as hell felt like he had.

He looked around; there was a plate of food and a pitcher of water with a glass on a small table beside the bed. He sat up gingerly and ate some of the now cold food. It tasted pretty good, nonetheless, and he downed the water almost in one draught, he was so parched.

He heard a noise out in the yard, and the door opened. Petey stood there with a broad smile on his little face, and a brown paper parcel in his hands. As soon as he saw his friend was awake, he ran over to him.

'Chase! You're OK! We was worried 'bout you. Sis sent your shirt back. I'll leave it here, shall I?'

He placed the parcel on the table, and stood looking down at Chase. Jake came in to the bunkhouse behind the boy.

'How long've I been out?' groaned Chase, rubbing at his bandaged wrists.

'Best part of two days and nights now,' replied Jake. 'We

got to wondering if we should call the doc out to you again. But it's good to see you're back with us, son. How you feelin'?'

'Ask me again in a week. I don't know if all my arms and legs are in their right places, my head hurts like hell, and my ribs feel like they've been tramped on by a herd of buffalo, but hey, I'm alive, so I guess I must be fine.'

'Who hit you, Chase?' Petey asked eagerly.

'Leave it, son,' Chase growled.

His head hurt real bad, he didn't really even want to have Petey chattering on at him, but he didn't want to upset the kid either. He knew Petey was just worried about him.

'Sis was cryin' cos you were bust up so bad, Chase. She told me it was just cos she had a fly in her eye, but it was when we were talkin' about you, so I think she was lyin'. Don't you?'

Jake smiled down at him, and placed his hand on the kid's shoulder.

'Women, eh, Chase? You never can tell what they really mean, kid.'

Chase was quiet; Sarah had been worried about him. Thinking about her made his heart ache almost as much as his ribs. He knew his ribs would heal, but would his heart?

As soon as his ribs had almost healed, Chase was back at Sarah's place one afternoon a week helping out as best he could. To Petey's delight.

And to Sarah's. She was beginning to enjoy having a man about the place to do the heavy jobs, and one who was as handsome as Chase Tyler was an added bonus.

CHAPTER ELEVEN

One afternoon Sarah decided to take Petey into Poynter for some supplies.

Chase wasn't with them that day. As he and Petey had done such a lot to make the place tidier, and make everything work better, there wasn't a great deal she needed to do around the place now.

She and Petey tacked up the old grey, and harnessed him to the buckboard. Slapping the reins, they set off at a trot towards town.

'D'you think we'll see Chase, Sis?' Petey asked, smiling.

'Doubt it, he's at the Parkers' place. Probably he won't be in town, but he'll be back at ours in a couple of days. You like him, don't you?' She smiled down at him sitting eagerly beside her.

'Yeah! He treats me like I was grown up, he talks to me like a man, not like a kid. And he doesn't shout at me if I get stuff wrong. He's the best!'

Sarah smiled to herself. She liked the man too, and had enjoyed watching the relationship between the man and boy developing over the weeks and months now, that he'd been around. But she knew, from talking to him and her few acquaintances in town, that he was a drifter. He'd soon be

128

riding out again.

Petey would get hurt. She would be hurt. Why he had hung around this long was a mystery; it had sounded like usually he lit out after a week or so at most. This time though, it seemed he had some sort of business to attend to, which was taking him quite a while longer. Well, Sarah didn't mind how long it took him; she enjoyed seeing him around. Like Petey, she'd grown quite fond of the man. For different reasons, of course.

It was a busy day in Poynter. Petey ran off to see if Chase was around the livery. Not finding him or Black there, he wandered around the town aimlessly, whilst Sarah collected her few supplies. She had just left the corn merchant, where the apprentice had loaded up the sacks into the buckboard for her, and was walking along towards the Murdochs' store, her last stop. She might ask a few questions about Chase whilst she was there, knowing that Annelise was his sister.

Bill left the store just as she arrived, tilted his hat in greeting, and held the door open for her. Annelise came out from the back room, carrying the baby.

'Hello, Mrs Jameson. Petey not with you today?'

'He's on the prowl, looking for Mr Tyler. He's grown quite fond of the man.' Sarah smiled.

Annelise, with that certain intuition given to most women, saw something behind that smile that made her think it wasn't just the boy who'd grown fond of her brother. And she quite liked Sarah and Petey. Maybe this time Chase might just realize that family life was a darned sight better than the drifter's life he'd been living up to now. She certainly hoped so.

Annelise could see how Chase had thought that Sarah was really Jess: her hair was similar, if darker, and so were her eyes, but Annelise knew, as did Chase if he thought rationally about it, that Jess had died in that awful fire. No one had survived; no one could have survived.

Chase was seeing ghosts, and his sister worried for him. But if, perhaps, this other woman could lay that particular ghost to rest, then maybe, just maybe, Chase would find his much needed peace at last.

Sarah placed her final provisions in the buckboard and looked around for Petey. Where was the boy? Trust him to disappear from sight just as she was ready to leave for home. She eventually spotted him, window-gazing at the saddler's up the street, and started to wander up to collect him. No point driving up there, their place was out in the opposite direction. She was in no great rush anyway.

As she strolled along the pavement, greeting the people she knew, Sarah became conscious that she was being watched. It wasn't Petey, he was still up ahead admiring the wonderfully tooled leather saddles. She looked around, maybe it was Chase watching her? She felt herself flush at the thought. No, he was nowhere in sight; anyway he'd have come over to her by now.

As she glanced about, a young man, leading a heavily loaded horse, stepped in front of her.

'Excuse me,' she said, trying to pass him.

He stepped into her path, and stood still, looking down at her. It was then that she noticed his arm was bandaged up and in a sling. She didn't like the look in his dark, deep, brown eyes.

'Can I help you, sir?'

He looked her up and down through those darkly glazed eyes, and leered down at her.

'Oh, I bet there's one hell of a lot you could help me with, lady.'

Shocked at the tone of his voice, she tried to push past

him, but again he blocked her path.

'You a friend of Chase Tyler, lady?'

She sighed with a kind of relief: he was a friend of Chase's. She thought she didn't much care for the sort of company he kept, but that was his business.

'He helps me out once in a while, yes.'

'When you see him next, give him a message from me, will you?'

'Sure, mister. Who shall I say you are?' She tried to back away, finding his presence rather uncomfortable now, but he matched her, step for step.

'No matter, he'll know all right. Just tell him, it won't just be his back he has to watch now.'

'I'm sorry? What do you mean?'

He reached out his hand towards her. She backed away again, only to be stopped by the front of a store. She drew her head back as his hand came closer. His fingers touched her cheek, and traced a light line down to her neck. He held them at her throat, for what seemed to Sarah like a very long moment, as he smiled darkly down at her. Then, abruptly, without another word, he turned, mounted his horse, and headed on out of town. Sarah watched him go, relieved and puzzled, her neck felt as though it was burning where his fingers had touched her. She shuddered.

She quickly went and fetched Petey, and they headed for home. Sarah was worried; the young man's message had sounded like a threat, but what did it mean? She really hadn't liked the way he'd touched her. There was a real coldness in his touch, and an even deeper coldness in his eyes. Should she go find Chase now, or wait a couple of days until he turned up at her place again?

The worry got the better of her, and she turned the horse in at the Parker ranch. Petey was puzzled.

'We goin' to look for Chase, Sis?'

'Sort of, Petey.'

As they approached the ranch house, she spotted Black in the corral; Chase must be somewhere close by. Good.

'Go see if you can find Mr Tyler in the bunkhouse or round about, tell him I need to see him,' she told Petey, who gladly jumped down and ran off to go and look for his friend. Jake Parker came out of the house. He looked surprised to see her.

'Howdy, Mrs Jameson. Don't usually see you around here. What can I do for you?'

'Is Mr Tyler about, please? Someone gave me a message to pass on to him.'

'Yeah, I think he's just in the bunkhouse, mendin' the stove.'

Sure enough Petey came out of the building with Chase in tow, wiping his hands on an old piece of cloth. She noticed that his face lit up when he saw her there.

'Mrs Jameson, good to see you. But what brings you out here?'

'I bumped into a young man in town – I mean, literally bumped into him, or he bumped into me. He wouldn't let me pass; he said he was a friend of yours, and he gave me a message to pass on to you. Oh, and he had his arm in a sling. Do you know him?'

Chase's blood ran cold; he'd thought Mitch would have been long gone by now. He tried to hide his concern, but his voice had gone as cold as ice.

'I know who he is. So what did he say to you?'

'He said I had to tell you, it won't just be your back you have to watch now. Do you know what he means, Mr Tyler?'

Chase and Jake exchanged glances. They both knew only too well what it meant.

'Sure I do. Thanks for deliverin' the message, ma'am. Nice to see you both today. I'll be over at your place Friday as usual. I've got to get on. 'Bye.'

He turned abruptly, and started towards the bunkhouse.

'Oh and, Mr Tyler, after conveying the message, he – well – he – touched me.'

He instantly whirled on his heels and came right back over to her, a deep frown on his handsome face.

'Touched you? How did he touch you? Did he hurt you in any way?'

Her heart leaped, he was concerned about her!

'He didn't hurt me, no, he just touched my cheek, kept his fingers on my throat, then he rode out of town. He was kitted up for a long ride, by the look of it.'

Chase hesitated. Should he go looking for the young whippersnapper, and end it now? He could be anywhere, though. It could take days, even weeks, to find the boy.

Chase had often been paid to find, and sometimes, even to kill, men, but now, well, this time at least, sense won out. It would be better for Sarah and Petey if he were to stick around, rather than go off on a wild-goose chase and maybe leave them in danger. He should have darned well finished the job when he'd had the chance. He cursed himself for letting the boy go, instead of killing him when he could. He couldn't let Sarah and Petey know what had gone on. Best to ignore it.

'Well, as long as you're OK, ma'am. It sounds like he's left town now, but if you should come across him again, you let me know, quick. Gotta go, work to finish. Be seein' yuh.'

He lifted his hand in an almost desultory wave, and turned back to the bunkhouse, leaving Sarah wondering what was going on. Petey quickly jumped up beside her.

'Chase is busy, Sis, can't stop his work today.'

She slapped the reins, annoyed at the man's cool response, and headed away from the homestead.

' 'Bye, Mr Parker,' she called as she turned the buckboard outside his house.

' 'Bye, ma'am. Hey, don't you worry 'bout Mr Tyler, he can take care of himself pretty well, you know. Be seein' yuh then.'

Sarah was driving away fast, and only heard part of what the older man had said. She was annoyed with the way that Chase had treated her. It had almost been as if she was a total stranger to him. As they rode along in silence, she dwelled on what had happened to her in Poynter.

It had been a threat to Chase, she realized that now. And probably to her and Petey also.

She could only hope that Chase would be sticking around for some time to come.

CHAPTER TWELVE

One clear morning, when his ribs had well healed, and he was more or less back to his normal self, Chase rode out to the border fence to start work on repairing the section he had previously left marked out.

He'd been hard at work for the best part of the morning when Black moved over towards him, pushed him gently on his shoulder, and whickered a low greeting. The stallion's eyes were fixed on the bend in the track. A cloud of dust was closing in on them fast.

Chase was curious. Black had sensed that whoever was coming in was posing no threat to them, and stood, ears pricked, nostrils flaring, bright eyes fixed on the dust cloud as it approached. Soon enough, Chase could see through the dust, and was able to recognize the long-toothed grey belonging to Sarah. The small rider on its back left him in no doubt that it was Petey who was riding it.

They were headed his way just as fast as the old grey cart-horse could gallop, and the boy was waving and shouting. Chase wasted no more time, and leaped quickly on to Black, sensing the urgency in the boy's flight. Chase urged the Morgan into a hard gallop towards the boy. He could hear the kid shouting as they drew closer.

'Mr Chase! Chase! Help! Come quick! It's Sis! She's hurt real bad! Come quick, please come!'

The two horses slid to a halt, side by side, in clouds of dust. Petey looked absolutely terrified. Tears streaked through the dirt and grime on his cheeks, his nose was running, his hair was standing up on end.

'Whoa there, son. Slow down and tell me what's happened. Where's your sis?'

'She's in our yard, but she's hurt bad. She was taking the yoke out with water for the corral and she caught her foot in the hound's chain. She went down real hard, Chase, real hard, and she's just lyin' there, and I can't make her wake up! I didn't know what to do, I remembered you said you were out here, so I just headed out, but she's all on her own and she might be dead!'

The boy paused and took a long sobbing breath. A fat tear rolled down his face, and he angrily swiped at it with his ragged sleeve.

'What if she's dead, Chase? What'll happen to me? Where'll I go? Can you come and help her. Please help her!'

The haunted, terrified, lost look in the boy's big blue eyes knotted Chase's throat up tight. He thought fast.

'Right, Petey, keep on goin', you get into town, and get the doc. I'll go see to your sis, she'll be fine. Go, as fast as this old nag will get you there. Tell the doc it's urgent, he's to come quick. Now *go*!'

He slapped the old horse on its rump. It took off like a whirlwind, the boy pulled its head round and swerved it back towards the town. Chase squeezed Black's sides hard; he hadn't stopped to saddle him up, so was riding bareback, and the horse could easily sense the real need for speed now. He set off like a striking rattler, almost leaving Chase behind, with a sudden leap forward.

136

As they drew close to the homestead, Chase could see Sarah, still lying on the ground. The heavy wooden yoke lay beside her. The water from the two buckets was pooling into a thick mud around her, and the big red hound was sitting close by. It leaped to its feet as the rider approached, and began to bark. Chase yelled at it to be quiet as they drew nearer, and it slunk back into its kennel.

It knew Chase well enough by now to know he would stand no nonsense. Chase leaped off Black even before the horse had skidded to a halt, and bent quickly over the prostrate woman. Thank God, she was still breathing. He was no doctor, but he checked her over for any obvious signs of life-threatening injuries. He pulled off his bandanna and quickly dipped it into the small amount of water which still lay in the bottom of one of the buckets.

Her blue poke bonnet had fallen off and was lying in the mud. Her hair had come unpinned, and the deep, auburn curls spilled around her pale face. Chase gently moved the soft tendrils to one side and placed the wet bandanna on her forehead.

He stood and swiftly shucked off his jacket, then tenderly covered the prostrate woman with it. Gently he patted her face.

'Ma'am? Miss Sarah? Ma'am? Are you OK? Speak to me, please. Please, ma'am, open your eyes for me.'

He wanted to pick her up, to take her into the comfort and warmth of her home, but he knew that, if she had broken anything, moving her could make it very much more serious; they needed to wait until the doctor came before he dared to move her.

But oh, how he wanted to take her into his arms.

He shook his thoughts back to the injured woman, soaked the bandanna again, and this time he squeezed it over her, so that some of the cool water trickled out from between his fingers down on to her face and into her eyes. To his great relief, she blinked as the water touched her face. She moaned softly, and stirred a little.

'Ma'am, wake up. Petey's gone for the doc. He's going to be here real soon now.'

Her eyes flickered open slowly. She looked up at Chase, who was kneeling, unheeding of his wet knees, in the mud puddle beside her. He reached out and took hold of her soft hand.

'That's right, Miss Sarah, you keep awake till the doc takes a look at you; he's on his way.'

Softly then, she squeezed his hand, and attempted to smile up at him. Chase's heart swelled up in his chest. He felt a warmth surge through his whole body. He felt like a kid again. Not since Jess had any woman had this sort of effect on him.

And now, more than ever, he was almost certain that this auburn-haired woman lying so unceremoniously in a pool of mud in front of him, was his own sweet Jess.

Soon they heard the sound of a buckboard being driven hard. Chase stood up. The doctor pulled up beside them. Petey was riding with him, and he leaped to the ground even before the wagon had stopped.

'Sis! Sis! You're awake! Are you OK? I thought you was dead!'

Petey made to give her a big hug, but Chase stopped him with a strong hand on his shoulder.

'Whoa, son. We've got to wait until the doc has a proper look at her. If there's any broken bones we don't want to make them any worse, do we?'

The boy shook his head energetically for no, a broad smile lighting up his grubby, tear-stained face. Chase looked around him.

'Petey, where's your ol' horse at?'

'I left her at the livery. She was plumb exhausted, never would have made it back here in time, and Fred said he'd look after her for us. I'll go get her later.'

He watched with Chase as the doctor checked Sarah over carefully. The doctor stood up and smiled at the man and boy beside him.

'This is getting to be quite a habit, me fetchin' up out here, isn't it? Well, luckily, she's got no broken bones, but it looks like she's got quite a badly twisted ankle. Mr Tyler, do you mind carrying her over into the house for me, please; we need to get her into some dry warm clothes and into her bed. She needs to rest.'

Chase hesitated for just a moment too long.

'It's fine, Mr Tyler don't worry, I'm here as chaperone, and as it's a medical emergency, no one will think it improper.'

Chase hadn't been worrying about that; it wasn't something that had even entered his head.

What was concerning him though, was picking up her small, fragile, body, and holding its soft warmth against him. He looked down at her and smiled, she smiled back weakly.

'Are you OK with that, ma'am?'

She nodded, her hair tangling in the sticky mud. Chase bent to pick her up. She winced as he lifted her from the mud; he almost dropped her back into it, afraid that he might be hurting her.

'It's fine, Mr Tyler. I'm all right, please carry on, the pain will soon go.'

She wrapped her arms around his neck, and closed her eyes. At the sudden touch of her warm flesh on his bare skin Chase momentarily closed his eyes also. The doctor spoke to Petey.

'Show us your ma's bed, boy, and find her night clothes for me, will you?'

'She ain't my ma, she's my sister, but follow me, Chase. I'll show you where she sleeps.'

Chase carried the woman carefully into the house, and followed Petey into a small, neat bedroom. He placed Sarah gently down on to the bed, and stepped back. His sharp, hunter's eyes took in all the details of the room. He was used to observing the smallest of details; you never knew when one small detail might come in useful.

It was neat and clean, as he would have expected it to be, with a minimum of furniture. A colourful patchwork quilt covered the bed, and a bright peg-rug lay beside it. A small night stand stood close to the bed with a bowl and a pitcher of water, beside which lay her brush and comb, and a bundle of brightly coloured ribbons.

Chase turned and left the room quickly, he felt uncomfortable somehow, being in her private place. And yet he so longed to stay there, immersing himself in her essence. As he left, Petey was showing the doctor the small set of drawers where Sarah kept her clothes.

Chase went over and sat at the table. Soon Petey came out and joined him. They sat together silently, each one deep in his own thoughts. Chase was more certain than ever that Mrs Sarah Jameson was really Jess McCloud. He'd have bet anything on it. He decided to face her with it, just as soon as she was back on her feet. Petey broke the silence.

'How'm I gonna look after Sis by myself, Chase? I'm just a kid. D'you think some of the ladies from town might come out to help us? Or maybe we could just take her over there, somebody might take her in for a while?'

'Strangely enough, that's about what I was thinkin', son. But I might just have another idea. How's about you and me looking after her right here?'

Petey stared up at him frowning.

'But how? You can't live in the house, there's no room, and anyway the townsfolk'd think it was improper if'n they found out.'

There were conventions to be obeyed, and a single man living in the same house as a woman on her own could well be misconstrued. That wouldn't help Sarah.

'But if'n I bed down in the barn, and you did most of the stuff in the house for her, and I did all the heavy stuff, it could work.'

The doctor came out then, and sat at the table beside them.

'Well, gentlemen, nothing's broken, but she does have quite a badly twisted ankle. It'll take a fair while for it to mend completely. She'll need to keep off of that foot as much as possible. I'll leave her a crutch to help her out, she should get about just fine with that. She'll be OK with some rest. I'll come over every once in a while to check on her, but if you have any problems at all, you just come and get me.'

Chase outlined his thoughts on the subject. The doctor was in complete agreement, and said he'd explain the situation himself to anyone who might get the wrong idea. Chase accompanied the older man out to the buckboard, where the doctor handed him out a crutch.

'I've left her some tablets for the pain too. They'll make her a bit sleepy for a while, but that's good. Just see she doesn't overdo the walking yet. And don't you worry 'bout the tattle-tongues out there, son: they'd be better coming out and offering their help, rather than gossiping about something that doesn't exist.'

'Thanks for that, Doc, we really do appreciate it, and thanks for coming out here so fast. What do we owe you?'

'You'll be coming into town to collect their old horse sometime, I expect?'

'Guess so, tomorrow I reckon.'

'We'll sort it out then. Just come into the surgery when you're passing.'

He climbed up on to the buggy seat and slapped the reins. As he moved off Petey ran out of the house.

'Sis says to thank you for your help, and for the tablets, Doc. Thanks.'

'Sure, son, it's fine. You look after your sister well now, y'hear?'

'I sure will, Doc. Me and Chase'll look after her real good. Thanks. 'Bye.'

The boy ran back inside, Chase waved the doctor off, and turned back to the house. After knocking on the door, he entered tentatively. Petey came out of his sister's room.

'If'n I'm goin' to be stayin' around here for a while, Petey, I'd best go over and get my gear from Jakes's place. It'll take me 'bout an hour or so. You be OK till I get back, son?'

'Sure, Chase. I think I can manage. Sis is sleepin' anyway right now. I guess those pills the doc left are workin.' If she wants anything I'll be able to help for a while till you get back.'

Chase whistled up Black, and leaped aboard, riding back towards the place where he'd been working earlier that day. On arriving back at the fence, he picked up the abandoned saddle, and saddled Black up. Then he headed towards the house.

He needed to tell Jake what was happening. He figured that the old man would be fine with his suggestion.

Chase would spread his time between the Double P and Sarah's place for a while now. Sarah would be fine in a few weeks, but right now she needed his help.

And Chase was going to do his best to help her, in any way, at any time, that he could.

CHAPTER THIRTEEN

Chase had been bedding down in Sarah's barn for a good couple of weeks, and with his and Petey's help she was getting around better with her crutch, and doing a little more cooking and cleaning around the place.

Chase shared the table with them at meal times, but he was careful never to go into the house unless invited, and always only when Petey was around. Some of the folk from town had called over occasionally, bringing food, or just for a visit and a chinwag with Sarah.

Chase had been spending part of his time over at Jakes's place; the rest of his time he spent in fixing Sarah's place up as best he could. He worked damned hard those weeks, most nights he slept, loglike, in his cot in the barn.

Sharing his time between Jakes's place and Sarah's was hard, but he was strong and fit, and his wounds were beginning to heal well now. He had begun splitting his nights between the two ranches now also.

As he worked at Sarah's place, he often felt her eyes on him, but usually, when he turned, she was nowhere to be seen, just the fleeting ghostlike shadow of her in the corner of his eye.

Young Petey was a real eager learner, always quick to run

about and fetch and carry for him, even taking the old grey horse into town some days to pick up provisions, or hardware that Chase or Sarah might need. He was soon mending many of the smaller items himself, running to Chase to show off his work, proud as could be of what he'd achieved.

And Chase was pleased for the boy in turn, it did his heart real good to see the joy on the boy's face when his mentor told him his work was good. Sarah was a darned fine cook, and Chase nearly always went back to Jakes's place with a parcel of cookies or a cake.

Sometimes though, when she didn't realize he was looking, Chase caught her with an expression of deep melancholy on her beautiful pale face. He couldn't help but wonder what had hurt her so much that it should leave its shadow on her for so long. He hated the thought of her ever being hurt. What had happened to her? Who had hurt her so much?

He couldn't bear the thought of her husband possibly beating up on her, like Jess's father had done to his wife and kids. Maybe that was why Sarah was so wary of men?

He knew, though, that he couldn't come right out and ask her. It wouldn't be proper. But then why the hell should it matter to him? But it did.

Chase had been trying real hard to avoid Sarah. He knew he was doing it, and he knew darned well why. He was so certain of her true nature that he found it extremely hard to keep his emotions in check whenever he got close to her. And of course, he couldn't come right out and challenge her with his suspicions. But there was just something about her, something which made him feel so protective towards her, in a way he thought he'd forgotten how to be.

One afternoon, he rode back from Jakes's place to Sarah's. As he approached he saw Petey, mounted on the old grey, in no great hurry, coming up the track towards him.

'Howdy, son. Where you off to? How's your sis today?'

'Sis is fine today, she was singin' this mornin.' She wants me to get some flour, she's run out and she wants to make some bread. See ya later, Chase!'

He rode off, and Chase rode into the yard, unsaddled, and let Black loose in the corral. He could see Sarah seated on the porch. He walked past her, making straight for the barn. Sarah's voice stopped him in his tracks.

'Mr Tyler, can you come over here for a while, please?'

She was sitting on the swing on the front porch, her crutch lying beside her. Her bonnet shaded her eyes even more under the cool shadow of the veranda. Chase cautiously approached her, wondering now whether sending Petey in to town had been some sort of an excuse on her part.

He couldn't help noticing, despite the shade, that she'd been crying, he could see that her cheeks were still damp. Chase took off his hat as he walked up the porch steps, and stopped at the top. He looked down at her quizzically, head cocked to one side.

'Ma'am?'

'Chase, please, come closer. I really need to talk to you.'

Her quiet use of his given name sent a shiver up his spine. He slowly took a few steps across the veranda towards her, the sound of his heels on the boards echoing around them like thunderclaps.

'Ma'am, you're upset. Is it my doin'?'

He stopped, a mere crutch-length away from her. His heart was beating so loudly, he thought she must be able to hear it from where she sat.

'In a way I suppose it is, yes, but also some of it is mine.' She sighed deeply, looking down at the ground.

Chase's heart lurched; he had never wanted to upset her. What was it he'd done? He shook his head and frowned. It was as if she had read his mind.

'No, it's nothing you've done, Chase. Oh, you don't mind me using your name, do you? But there is something that I do need to talk to you about, and I've really got to say it now, before my courage fails me again.'

He shook his head when she mentioned his name; of course he didn't mind her using it, he loved to hear her use it. She motioned to the old rocking-chair.

'Please sit, so I can see you properly, you're so tall.'

He dragged the chair round to face her, and sat down, holding his breath, leaning in towards her, waiting to hear what she was going to say. The ruby curls tumbled from beneath her bonnet, curling crazily around her shoulders. His eyes took in every curl and wave. His fingers itched to reach out and touch them.

'Chase. I'm so very sorry. I've been lying to you. And to Petey. To everyone. For such a long time. I just can't do it any more.'

She shook her head, took a deep shuddering breath, and a tear ran down her cheek. He wanted to go over and wipe it away. He wanted to kiss it away. She seemed not to notice it.

'I don't understand, ma'am? Lying? To everyone? How?'

'Oh Chase, I can't go on this way any longer. I've battled with myself for so long, trying to decide how to tell you and Petey. Especially poor Petey. He's gotten so close to you lately, and having you coming round here so often this past few weeks, has just made it so much worse in one way. So that's why I decided: you both have to know, now.'

Chase was scared. She was ill, she was trying to tell them she was dying. He'd lose her again. He pulled himself

147

together; he was aware he was panicking, not thinking straight. He took a deep shuddering breath, held it, and waited for her next sentence.

The silence went on for so long; she was crying quietly; he desperately wanted to put his arms around her.

'Please, ma'am – Sarah, tell me what's wrong. I can tell young Petey for you if you want.'

'That's the first problem, you see. Everyone calls me ma'am, but I'm not actually married. Never have been. Just used any name to make myself respectable. A married woman with a child, even without her husband around, is a darned sight more respectable than an unmarried woman with a child, isn't she?'

'Well, yes, I reckon so, ma'am, but that's no worry as far as I'm concerned. Anyway, Petey's your little brother, not your son, so where's the problem?'

'That's another thing. You see, he's really not my brother. He is actually my son. I've just reared him to believe he's my kid brother. Told everyone he was. I reckoned it was better for him that way. And I . . . I. . . .'

Chase's mind was whirling.

'There's something else?'

'Oh Chase. The fire. I didn't die. I'd run away that night. I panicked and went off up north. But Petey . . . he—'

'Why? What are you sayin?'

His heart was hammering, he felt sure she could hear it now.

'Chase, you are right. It is me. Jess. I'd found out that I was pregnant that week. I knew that if Pa found out, he'd kill me first, then he'd kill you, slowly and painfully. I just had to get away. I didn't dare tell you. I couldn't risk Pa killing you, I loved you so much. It nearly broke my heart to have to do it. I only found out about the fire that killed them all a year or so later.'

'Pregnant? But then Petey. . . ?'

'Yes Chase, Petey. He's your son. He's our son.'

She whispered so quietly, her voice was all but inaudible.

'But why not come back here sooner? Your pa was dead; he couldn't hurt us any more. You must have known I'd be coming home every so often to see Annelise. Why not come back before? Why not tell 'Lise? Why be the mystery woman? Why the hell not tell me before now, Jess, when I told you I knew?'

He was angry now; why had she betrayed him? He jumped up from the chair and began to pace up and down the veranda, clenching and unclenching his fists. Wanting to hit something.

Wanting to hold her. She took a deep and shuddering breath.

'Oh Chase, I wanted to come back so often, I really did. But I was so very afraid that everyone might think it was me who'd burnt down the house, so I decided it would be best to wait. I needed to get work, I had to save up enough money to come back here, and buy a small place for me and Petey to live, it took a long time. Much, much longer than I had expected, and by the time I did get back here, we'd settled into the sister, brother thing, and I honestly didn't know how to tell 'Lise then, I couldn't. And I'd heard you'd been drifting since the fire, doing things that maybe weren't quite legal. Horrible things sometimes.'

She shuddered, and a tear ran down her face to her pale neck, Chase watched the track of it as it disappeared beneath the collar of her light-blue blouse. He was shaken back to the moment, when she began to speak again.

'But I still wanted to find you again, Chase, that was why I came back, so that one day we'd meet again. That's why all

the mystery, why I kept everyone at arm's length. Why I darkened my hair. I had to tell you first. But I really didn't know
how. I didn't know when you'd be back here again. It was so
hard. The waiting. Then, oh, seeing you again, and being
afraid to let you know too soon, before I knew if I still felt the
same way for you. And I do. Oh Chase, I'm so very sorry.
Forgive me. Can you? Please?'

The silence was tangible. His head was spinning. He'd
been right all along. It really was Jess. But Petey? His son? He
walked away from her. That explained the feeling of fondness he'd had towards the boy almost as soon as they'd met.

He went across to the barn and sat on a hay bale, head in
his hands. It was such a lot to take in. What the hell should
he do?

Some long, silent minutes later he marched purposefully
back to the house. Jess was still sitting where he'd left her.
She watched as he walked towards her. She couldn't read his
expression. He took the porch steps two at a time, sat on the
swing beside her, and took her in his arms at last.

As he pulled her close to him, and felt the fragile warmth
from her slender body, all of the frustration, desire, and
pent-up passions and emotion of the last twelve years
flooded through him. His heart soared. He wanted to take
her, right there. But he knew it could ruin everything. He
had to take it slowly, take care, bide his time. But oh, was it
going to be hard.

He was never going to let go of her now. He'd lost her
once, he certainly wasn't going to lose her again. He held on
to her so tightly, she squealed.

'Chase! Not so tight! Please. You'll break my ribs!'

He quickly let her go, apologizing profusely, making her
laugh at his discomfiture.

'Jess! After all these years. All the pain. My God, Jess, it really is you? It is you? I knew!'

'Oh Chase, you can't know how hard it's been these last weeks, watching you work, and not being able to tell you that it really was me. I've wanted to. Every day I've tried to find a way, but I was so afraid of what you'd think of me if I did. And of what would happen to Petey. Oh Chase, what's going to happen to us now?'

He put his arm around her and smiled broadly.

'Well, I guess we're goin' to have to tell everyone. I told 'Lise it was you when I first saw you again, but she laughed at me, told me there were thousands of women who looked like you. Hundreds with hair like you, hundreds with kid brothers too. But I knew.'

'You mean you don't mind?'

'Mind? Oh Jess, I've thought about you almost every day. I've dreamed of you almost every night. I told you way back then, I'd never stop loving you, and I never have. I've hoped against hope, every week since then, to see you again, and marry, and raise a family with you. It's kept me goin' in some pretty rough situations, I can tell you. And now it's all here at last, it's all real. Marry me, Jess?'

'Oh Chase, you don't know how long I've hoped to hear those words. Yes I will. Oh yes!'

Without any more words, they clung to one another tightly. Chase tilted her head up, and slowly, gently, kissed Jess at last. Tears rolled down both of their faces, but their smiles were broad. They kissed hotly. Then Jess pulled away.

'Who's going to tell Petey, though? And how? He'll take it pretty hard.'

'What? That I'm really his pa?' Chase laughed.

'No, you silly mule well, maybe that too, but the fact that he's always looked on me as his sister, and now he's going to have to start calling me Ma! He'll be so confused, poor kid!'

'Yeah, It'll take him some getting used to, but I reckon he'll be fine with it all, and it won't take him too long to adjust. He sure is a fast learner! Just like his pa!'

They laughed together, cried together, and held on to one another, tightly, fiercely, as if they were drowning.

'So, who tells Petey then?' Jess smiled up at him, her emerald eyes filled with tears.

As if at a signal, they spotted the old grey horse coming back up the track. Black whickered a greeting, and the grey replied.

'We'll both tell him.' Chase replied, taking her hand in one of his, and gently wiping at her tears with the thumb of his other hand. As Petey dismounted in the yard, Chase called out to him.

'Petey, come over here, son, we want to talk to you for a minute.'

Chase felt his throat catch as he used the word 'son', because now it had a completely different meaning to him.

Petey took a little while to adapt to the fact that his sister was really his mother, and that his best friend, Chase, was really his real father, but soon enough he was excitedly telling the whole story around town, to anyone who'd listen.

Chase and Jess spent most of that night locked in one another's arms. There was such a lot to catch up on. They told one another everything they could think of about how they had led their lives in the intervening years. Chase shamefacedly told her of the times he'd either been paid, or simply had to, out of self-defence, kill other men. She understood. She wasn't happy about it, but she understood, and made him promise that he would undertake no more killing.

He hesitated; he knew he might have to use his gun again. It was a dangerous world out there, but he promised her he would definitely try. That was the best he could do for her. She smiled at that, knowing he really meant it. He would never do anything to hurt her.

Chase went with Jess and Petey to Murdoch's store to give them all the news. He apologized to Annelise and to Bill. His sister's earlier tirade had served to make him see the real truth of his bad feelings toward his brother-in-law: it had been pure jealousy on Chase's part.

There was nothing bad about Bill at all, he was just a good, hardworking, and extremely shrewd businessman, and although the two men would never be the best of friends, an uneasy truce was at last declared between them.

Annelise was totally thrilled when Chase and Jess told her they were to marry, and the children and Petey were absolutely delighted to find out that they were really cousins. They all went out to play together in the yard as the adults talked.

The wedding, later that year, was a fancy affair. Jess and Chase had wanted to keep it small and quiet, but Annelise would have none of it, and, with the help of her lady friends, arranged one of the best 'do's' that had been seen in the area for a long time.

Annelise offered to make sure Petey was OK whilst Chase and Jess went to Jonesville for their honeymoon. Even Bill entered into the spirit of the day, and had a drink with Chase.

As they pulled away in the beribboned buggy, with Black in the harness; Jess and Chase waved at the folks who'd gathered. Chase pulled Jess towards him and kissed her hotly, to a rousing cheer from the crowd. The future was looking pretty fine for Chase Tyler right now.

But all the time, in the back of his mind, there lurked the worry that somewhere out there was a cold, vengeful, killer, who had a grudge against him.

He'd need to keep his senses well honed from now on. He had a family to protect now.

CHAPTER FOURTEEN

Jess huddled in close to Chase as Black trotted along the track towards Jonesville.

Chase couldn't remove the silly grin from his face. Jess was his at last. After all the years of pain and longing, needing and searching for . . . who knew what? She was here in his arms. She was his wife! And most unexpectedly, and just as good, was the fact that Petey was his son.

The only regret he had now though, was that they had not been together through those years, and grown as a family. But there would be many years together now, many years for him to teach Petey and get to know him. And to get to know Jess properly again.

He laughed out loud, from the pure joy of the moment. It was infectious; soon they were both laughing until the tears were rolling down their faces. He couldn't remember when he had ever been so happy. Certainly not for a great many years.

As their laughter subsided, Chase noticed that Black was looking a little skittish. His gait had changed, he was holding back for some reason. Chase looked up. Up ahead on the trail, a solitary rider was heading their way. Slowly sauntering, not rushing, taking his time. But as he drew nearer, Jess drew in her breath.

'Chase, it's that *hombre* who gave me the message in town!'

'Yeah, I know, honey.'

The fact that the rider wore his arm in a sling made it obvious who it was. Mitch. Smiling broadly. Looking like a wolf on the hunt. As the distance between them lessened. Chase whispered to Jess,

'When I say so, Jess, you get down as low as you can, as fast as you can.'

She opened her mouth to ask something. Chase snapped at her.

'No questions! Just do it!'

She looked at him, her face paled, her bright eyes widened in fear. She hadn't seen this side of him before. Hard, cruel, eyes like steel, jaw twitching. She knew better than to argue though, whilst at the same time knowing that he wasn't going to let anything hurt her.

As they drew closer, Mitch touched the brim of his hat. Chase noticed he wore just one gun, but he was suspicious of the sling the boy was wearing.

'Nice seein' you again, ma'am, Mr Tyler.'

'Wha'dya want, Mitch? I thought I told you to disappear!'

'Oh, now, Chase. Is that any way to talk to a guy who's come to wish you and your new bride a happy marriage? I heard the news. My congratulations to you both.'

Jess smiled down at him, he sounded sincere. She was in a happy mood, despite the tension she could feel filling the air.

'Thank you, mister,' she said.

Chase nudged her. 'Shhhh.'

Mitch shook his head, tutting slowly,

'Tyler, Tyler, Tyler, that ain't no way to behave towards an old friend, is it? Your lady is more polite than you.'

He was riding slowly around them now. Chase stood up in the well of the buggy, turning as the rider turned around them, flexing his muscles, readying himself for what he knew, only too well, was about to come.

'Now then, Tyler, how best to congratulate you both, I wonder?'

Chase's sharp gaze noticed the smallest movement of Mitch's good arm, towards the sling which held his other arm.

'What do you have in mind, Mitch? Are you calling me out?' Chase growled. His eyes narrowed. Jess began to worry, her gentle lover was changing into a beast right before her eyes.

'Chase, please,' she whispered.

'Get down!' he shouted.

Instinctively, she dropped to a crouch at his feet as Mitch drew a gun from within the sling and aimed a shot at Chase. As he tried to pull the revolver clear, though, the metal caught on the edge of the fabric, and the shot went wild.

Chase fired a return shot. Mitch ducked, the bullet missed its mark. Mitch swore loudly as he took aim once again at Chase. The gun flew from his fist then, as Chase's second bullet grazed his knuckles. Mitch then quickly went for the gun that was hanging in his belt, and drew on Chase, dark brown evil shining from his eyes.

Chase was faster.

Mitch hit the floor beside his mount with a dusty thud, and a bullet in his heart.

Jess screamed. Chase dropped to his knees beside her, pulling her into his arms, pressing her to his chest, holding her tightly.

'I am so sorry you had to see that, my love.'

'Oh Chase, he would have killed us both, I could see it in

157

his eyes.'

'He would. With no qualms either. And left us for the buzzards. He's a no-good sonofabitch who tried to kill me three times, and then bushwhacked, and beat me, that time you helped me. I tried to give him the chance to turn his life around by letting him go, but his mind had just gotten too warped with thoughts of revenge.'

'Is this the life you live, Chase? Is this what we have to live with from now onward?'

The tears flowed freely as she buried her face in his shirt. He held on to her tightly. He'd not wanted her to see anything of that life. It was all behind him now. With Jess and Petey by his side he would be a changed man. She was sobbing and shaking.

'You promised me, Chase. You promised me,' she said quietly, not looking at him.

'Loose ends, Jess. Loose ends, that was all. It's over now There'll be no more. No more. But we really do have to carry him into Jonesville; we can't leave him out here. The sheriff can take our statements, and wire Poynter. Sheriff Thomas and plenty other people can vouch for me, and the fact that Mitch was gunning for me. There won't be any problem.'

He jumped down, and busied himself in tying Mitch's horse to the buggy. He hoisted the boy's body into the rear and covered it with some sacking. Slowly then, he approached the front of the buggy, looking down at the floor.

'Jess, this used to be what my life was like. Simply because you weren't in it, my love. Had you been, I would have taken a different road. I will be taking that other road now. All of this is behind me. It is all finished at last, because of you.'

'Promise me, Chase, that you won't kill any more. No

more killing, Chase?'

'No more killing, Jess. Save, if needed, as any man would, to protect my family. I promise this with my life. No more needless killing.'

He jumped up beside his new wife; they held on to one another tightly. She pushed him away gently, held him at arm's length, and looked up into his eyes, hard and long.

Gone was the hard steeliness, the coldness of the killer she had just seen.

His eyes were soft, gentle, and contrite. He was telling her the truth. She knew that. And she believed him. He slapped the reins.

'Walk on, Black. Unfortunately, we've a rather unpleasant task to perform on our first wedded day, let's get it over with as quickly as we can, then we can begin to live our new life together.' Jess squeezed his arm hard, and looked up into those shining, bright-blue eyes.

'No more killing, Jess, I promise you.'

'I trust you, Chase,' she said. He smiled down at her, knowing he'd never been happier. But would he be able to keep his promise?